# DREAM
# STATE

BOOKS BY MOIRA CRONE

*The Winnebago Mysteries and Other Stories*
*A Period of Confinement*

# DREAM STATE

STORIES

Moira Crone

University Press of Mississippi / *Jackson*

The paper in this book meets the
guidelines for permanence and durability
of the Committee on Production
Guidelines for Book Longevity of the
Council on Library Resources.
Library of Congress Cataloging-in-
Publication Data appear on page 190.

These stories appeared in the following
publications in slightly different form:
"Oslo" in *The New Yorker*, "Fever" in
*Missouri Review*, "There Is A River in New
Orleans" in *Negative Capability*, "I Am
Eleven" in *Short Story*, "Crocheting" in
*Washington Review of the Arts* and in the
anthology *American Made*, "Dream State"
in *The Gettysburg Review*, and "Gauguin"
in *The North American Review*.

"Dream State" won the 1993 Pirate's Alley
Faulkner Society Award for short story.
Excerpts from the story first appeared in
their publication *Double Dealer Redux*.

My thanks to the editors of all these
magazines and especially to Rosemary
James and Joseph DeSalvo and to Richard
Abel and JoAnne Prichard of the
University Press of Mississippi.

I would also like to thank the Mary
Ingraham Bunting Institute of Radcliffe
College, the National Endowment for the
Arts, and the Charles Manship Fund at
Louisiana State University for their
generous support during the time that I
wrote these stories.

*For my favorite dreamers—*
*Rodger, and my girls, Anya and Kezia*

# CONTENTS

VII

# DREAM STATE

# DREAM STATE

I'm assuming you know who Jessica Broussard is.

I just saw her this afternoon. She doesn't look like anybody now, after what she's been through—Julian, L. A., that house—but I notice her. You can't undo the past.

The first time she calls me, she says, "Beryl Jackson?" with the faintest Louisiana accent, something she never got a chance to use on screen. I know immediately. Of course I've heard a lot of things already—not just the stuff in the supermarket magazines. People in St. Sebastianville have been telling me she isn't from a "good family," right after they proclaim they've known her all their lives, always knew she'd be a star.

"H. J.—H. J. Birney? says I should work with you. I'm looking for a house . . ." she goes on. She is the incredible plum he's sent my way to keep me on. He's losing his agents in droves just then.

She suggests we go to Pegue's. The place is a dive: a shack next to a big yard full of poured concrete garden ornaments—statues of angels, pelicans, St. Francises, little lambs. But this is a rule I am learning. In dives down here the cooks can be geniuses. I love it. We have shrimp remoulade, pan-sauteed soft-shell crab. She is wearing Lycra leggings—this is long before everybody does. When she takes off her sunglasses, the whole room turns around.

Actually, even very near the end, we still go to that little place off and on, for a snatch of gumbo, some étouffée. It changes. So do we. Later, people turned around less readily. I guess those last days she just wanted to make sure her secrets were safe with me. Well, they are—this is what I'm saying, I think. There's the matter of what people can bear to hear, to even know.

H. J. told me when I went to work for him that people in St. Sebastianville hate black clothes and the word "no." Black is too depressing, no matter what *Vogue* says. The best color to wear to sell is periwinkle blue. It is the eighties. I say yes.

At Pegue's I nod my head when Jessica says she wants to buy something "simple." She has a California mind-set. She assumes a little plain brick suburban place will cost a quarter million.

I wish.

She is hiding out, as I see it, in exile from L. A., home-to-her-roots, based on research I've done watching "Entertainment Tonight." There is the harassment thing, her children's father suing her two years after the original palimony settlement—rumored to be vast—calling her obsessed, unstable. He's accused Jessica of four-in-the-morning phone calls, leaving voodoo dolls on his doorstep, little miniatures of his new love, a starlet, pierced through the heart. Some producers have said she "won't work in Hollywood again." Everybody has denied everything, except the starlet, who is always on TV.

Do you remember any of this?

Never once do I ever ask Jessica to explain.

The year is 1985. Louisiana Sweet (that's oil, really—a perfect contrast, I think, to Texas Crude, so descriptive, Texas *is* crude) fell below twenty dollars a barrel a little before we moved here. So people are going broke. Real estate has collapsed. The least serious brokers have fled first—the pert mothers of four (Catholic, inconceivably trim), next, the retirees, then the young blazer guys, and finally the peach fuzz boys fresh from L. S. U. I'm new to Louisiana, in none of these categories.

"Hold on, y'all," I remember H. J. telling us about this

time. "I called up my grandfather about this. You have to go back to the thirties." His family can be traced to the dawn of St. Sebastianville. "Deflation. That's the enemy. Everything can go down to the price of dirt. Not a pretty sight. We have a mission, here, a raison d'être, it's interesting again. Don't let anybody panic . . . esprit . . ."—his speech to the three of us who are still coming to sales meetings.

I am thinking, I have never seen anyone so complex running a real estate company. He goes off into French, quotes Montaigne.

"What we need now is confidence. Beryl, don't leave us, cher."

He believed in me because he thought I was from the North, and therefore I had energy. I'm not from anywhere, but if you are from nowhere here they call it the North.

So, even though she says she wants something boring, I show the movie star Jessica Broussard the biggest nicest house we are listing. A heavy columned extravaganza on the lake. "I can have this?" she asks me as we drive up. "This is so strange. When I was a little girl, I thought gods lived here."

It is a copy of the plantation homes nearby on the river, but adapted, jazzed up, serviceable, lots of hosta and monkey grass, azaleas and banana trees in the front. It dates from the

1930s. On the second floor are those tall, narrow louvered shades—long, long eyelashes, to shade the balcony. I still love those, can't get enough of them.

"You know what Amanda Potter said to me the other day?" Jessica remarks when we walk up to the house.

Like I know who Amanda Potter is. I act as if I do.

"She took me to the St. Sebastianville Hotel, and when I took off my hat, she said, all serious, like this was a revelation, 'You look the same.' "

"Well, you look really beautiful," I say, impressed how normal I am being with somebody who has kissed Dennis Quaid.

"No, that's not really it. It's as if I have to have changed somehow. When I haven't. I haven't. You get it?"

"Yes, yes, I do," I say.

She goes through the house really quickly—she doesn't even look—and then she asks me to let her out onto the side patio with the view. You are supposed to stay with the client. So I follow.

I open the iron gate for her and let her go ahead—give her some space. She sits on one of the teak benches—they are staying, I think of mentioning. Pointing at one of the mansions across the water, she asks me who lives there.

When I tell her Julian Pendergrast who owns a restaurant,

she says, loudly, "I know who Julian Pendergrast is." She seems agitated, even saying his name.

I tell her he has recently bought one of the real plantation homes, one of the places on the river, Camellia Hill, ca. 1845, to renovate. There are all sorts of rumors what he is going to do with it—maybe a guest house, or just something very grand for him and his family—he's been making a killing, even in these hard times, with his restaurant. H. J. is thrilled about this project of Julian's, what it will mean for values. So I know quite a bit. I am still snowed by H. J. Birney at this point in my life.

She says, sort of to the air, "That sounds just like something Julian would do."

As if on cue, she snaps out of her little spell and comes back to the front porch. "Do you like this house?" I ask after an amount of time I think is cool.

"It's like a fat woman crouching on the beach," she says.

"Botero calves," I say, this just comes out, I mean the squat Spanish Colonial pillars on the first floor.

"Yes, yes, yes," she says, sitting down on the front steps, laughing really hard. "I love Botero, don't you? His people are so *intense*." She opens her eyes extra wide to say that last word. This is marvelous to watch. How can I say it: the way she opens her eyes so much wider makes me feel there is more in her head.

"I know what you mean," I say, trying to. We sit there for a while and stare out into the gray-green lake, full of snowy egrets perched on top of cypresses that are still alive—in the country bayous my husband, Randall, has lately taken me to see, the pollution has killed these trees, but here there is a weak cypress perfume-like breeze. I kind of forget who Jessica is. But even in the way I forget, I feel special.

I was an Air Force brat growing up, never lived anywhere long enough to learn from my mother how to keep a house, much less the difference between a Queen Anne and a Greek Revival. I drifted into real estate in Washington during those Carter years, the early Reagan expansion. I had a degree in art history, but the money was in houses. Those were the days when people bid past the asking price the first morning a three-bedroom in Bethesda hit the market. But I wasn't sorry about D. C., about leaving there. It was a big train station, I thought, like everywhere else I'd ever lived. But here we'd arrived in Louisiana, the Dream State, that was what the bumper stickers they handed out at the tourist center on the state line read.

When we hadn't been here a month—we'd come down because Randall got a job in environmental law—I insisted we take two local house tours. The first plantation was from the 1700s. A Frenchman lived there, had a million children. He was an aide de camp of Lafayette. But the story wasn't revolution. Freedom had nothing to do with it. It was bolts, and keeping the Indians away and surviving malaria and locking up the knives so the slaves couldn't get them, and putting the tea and the spices under a board in the floor, and occasionally, the wives and daughters being burned alive when the fire under the kettle caught their petticoats. Of course, as always, babies dying fast as flowers, mothers too. The whole story the docent told—she was a sweet little woman, with a fairy godmother sort of bearing, a long dress, a little cloth cap on her bun—was danger, white people who would stop at nothing to keep it at bay, all for the sake of grand appearances, a few modest rooms with fleur-de-lis stencilling, some silver, some painted floorcloths. All the owner's letters, displayed in a little glass box, were about yearning, how he had to return to France, how his heart ached, how he dreamed of home.

He never got back.

"This place gives me the creeps," Randall said.

I found it romantic, Gallic, tragic.

The next place was a little strange—a big Riverboat Gothic surrounded by a high electric fence, on the grounds of an enormous chemical plant on the Mississippi. We were told that in the 1850s a speculator could make a million—a nineteenth-century million, mind you—in cotton in five years with a few thousand slaves, and build a castle. "Vinyl chloride," was all Randall had to say about that incredibly grand, gilded place. He was talking about the smokestacks outside, the white puffs, a recent history of lethal silver ash dusting the towns downwind. He said something else pretty nasty—comparing plantations and corporations—which I didn't really want to hear at the time. He made me mad, really. I thought he missed the beauty. I couldn't get Randall to see any other houses so I went by myself, after that, soaked up the lore like an orphan visiting a happy family, hoping someday I'd have a use for it, go inside some of the show-places without having to buy a ticket.

Because it's been so long, I ask again if Jessica's interested, there on the front porch. "Oh, it's a great house," she says, "but I don't want to get that close to Julian. You must know."

I assume she means they were lovers once. I act like I know of course. "I see," I say, trying to sound southern, complex.

Then she gets back in my car and asks me to just drive.

Her wish, as they say. We go through St. Sebastianville—the old downtown, the black neighborhoods, the junior highs surrounded by fences of aluminum link and barbed wire, NO FIREARMS ON THE PREMISES signs, past the lakes and the Love River and the developments where people who are nobody would live—engineers for the plants on the river, people like Randall and me, and well, she sees one of those meaningless houses has a red white and blue H. J. Birney sign, with our slogan: "Gracious living, at affordable prices."

She tells me, brakes.

It seems like cheating, the way I can look so hard at her in that late afternoon sun when we get out of the car. No filter. No lenses. She is beautiful. With her in it, a dull neighborhood like that doesn't seem like life, anymore, it seems a perfected replica, done by an art director. She has an almost ingenue Ava Gardner appeal, and such slender hands. And the kind of legs you can't get over how thin they are. They fold under her easily as a blanket when she sits on the stoop, while I fiddle with the key to the lock box. I am so nervous. Her head is really huge in relationship to her body, which gives her some of the quality of a doll. I have this revelation, looking at her, that's she's going to be my raison d'être—I'll have one, like H. J. and even Randall. This is my cause: Jessica Broussard, the difficult star, finding her a place in the world.

But this house is one dull bloated Cajun rancher. High roof, cathedral ceiling. She signs a contract on it that very afternoon. I don't even have time to talk her out of it, to get persuasive.

The development is called Bayou Arms.

"What happened?" H. J. asks me. "She's a millionaire. It's peanuts. *Palmetto* alone (she was a vamp in *Palmetto*, stole another woman's husband) grossed 90 million—Beryl? You there, cher?" He looks at me, with his suddenly boyish disappointment.

I really don't know what has happened. She has bought a house exactly like a thousand other houses. It isn't even a good buy.

After Jessica moves in, I deliver the firm's good neighbor package—a copy of our gumbo cookbook, a little sago palm in a pot. She just lets me in and says not a word, as if that first Botero afternoon had never happened. Her new house is a mess—cheap futons are the furniture, Legos and baby dolls all over the floor. She is sitting on a pillow playing crazy eights with her two little children, Juliana and Sebastian, their heads bristly with L. A. haircuts. She is living like a refugee, as they say. My fault.

"B-?" she says to me.

"Beryl?" I ask her.

"Bye," she says.

Talk about exile.

Talk about being kicked out of Eden.

Oh, I live without her. Exist, is more like it.

This is the fall of 1985, the spring of 1986. I show those turkeys, the Ponderosas, 4.2 acres, two satellite dishes, boat ports, kitchens with miles of pickled cypress, little chandeliers everywhere, even in the laundry room. Tammy Faye taste. H. J. writes the ads, says these monsters have "amenities galore"—I can't bear it. These are the ones that have been on the market the longest—built by the people who have never had money before, made millions in the oil boom, and lost theirs first. I am just keeping up appearances, doing open houses, asking four hundred thousand when the truth is those sellers will take anything—they are ready to pay the buyers to take on the notes. Before I go out to show these places, H. J. corners me like a playground bully.

"Got it, Beryl? Nobody dumps."

For a while the only traffic is the curiosity seekers— "Come look, Maggie! Mirrors on the bathroom floor!" Like everybody else, I am thinking of leaving the state, or finding a paying job, if there are any.

Jessica is incognito those months—almost a year. Nobody knows what she's been doing over there in Bayou Arms, although people never stop asking. It is significant, I guess, though, that as long as she lives there, nobody goes to find out. Not even me. It is just too weird—too contrary to expectations—that a movie star would live in such a place. It is like an error.

Mine.

So I don't go.

Randall is busy as he can be—his work is cut out for him. We haven't made up our minds about children yet—we really don't have that much time to talk about it. What can I say, we have a pasta machine, a rowing machine, a cappuccino machine. We eat out of cartons, off salad bars, from microwaveable bags. It is that time in human events. Life is elsewhere.

Then, in the fall of 1986, in the very darkest days, when the housing inventory is mounting, no end in sight, I get a message on my tape . . . "Beryl? Remember me?"

I call right back.

"I need something nicer. More privacy, maybe. Can we go look? I'm open." Oh, that gravel in her voice. Unmistakable. More privacy? She hasn't seen a soul in a year. I know for a fact.

But I am alive. Reborn.

We look at everything on the market: she doesn't have a "price range." This is something more than a material pursuit. The inventory is wild by then. We are at the second wave of bankruptcies. The best wave, as far as I'm concerned. We see all the mansions: the fake plantations of convicted felons, of famous football players whose businesses have collapsed in a general avalanche of shady deals, of judges from ancient families who have gotten caught. Jessica loves the gossip. She gives me lots of her own, about the producer she had her babies by. I find out the real reason she's gotten so much money from him. The perfidy. Why he really had to settle out of court. This stuff is delicious, fascinating. In this version, nobody is really bad, just confused, thoughtless. "It's just like everybody says it is," she says to me about L. A. "Everything is for sale. You wouldn't believe. People make appointments months in advance to fuck, put it in the contract." This is one afternoon when we were trying to figure out if a certain couple who have put their updated Acadian on the market are still sleeping together. As long as I am her confidant, I have confidence. She will buy something really marvelous, really right. I know it. I am so high.

"Nobody in California knows what beauty is," she says to me one day, when we are at Pegue's, gobbling heavenly boudin. "They don't really know how to eat, either."

"I know," I say. "Nobody anywhere anymore."

"Except maybe here," she says. "Huh?"

The cement garden there looks great then, spectacular. Everything does, the whole day. The day after.

I've been dropping a few names. "So what's Jessie think Kathleen Turner's really like?" Randall says one morning at breakfast. It so happens it's the day I am going to show Jessica the Botero again—of course it is still for sale. I've been showing her houses for about a month and a half. She's said she's finally decided. She's asked me to bring a blank contract. It is October. It's my big day.

And Randall is making fun of me.

"I don't need this," I tell him.

When I get over there, I notice the owners have left potpourri in every room. Since Jessie despises it, I go back through and hide every bowl in a drawer or under a sink. *Scent can make all the difference in a sale,* I've been told in a seminar. *Tell the owner to bake cinnamon cookies before he leaves the house.* Then I go back and sit in my car. She's supposed to meet me at three. I listen to "Fresh Air." And the first half-hour of "All Things Considered."

No Jessica.

No beauty.

Ninety-two minutes later I go inside and call the office. And Randall at work. At Jessica's a maid answers.

She's flown out to L. A. with her kids. She's gone. Like that. Wham.

"She's temperamental," H. J. tells me the next day. "Don't you read the movie magazines?"

"Now you say," I say.

Then he shrugs—"Who, me?"

I actually feel guilty, not jilted.

"We need her," he says later on, more than once. Then he looks over at me. "Think what she could do for us—what Walker Percy does for living in Covington."

I go along, blame myself for her leaving—for ever letting her buy that place at Bayou Arms, which surely made her miserable. Outside the firm, some people tell me if she comes back we should try to get her to come out and appear—"be a figure locally"—is the way they put it. Others say she should stay in Hollywood. People start to address me in groups whenever Jessie comes up. This is good for business, what business there is.

"Now you look like her sister!" Randall says, when I get my hair cut really short. I feel better, what can I say, when I do this. I guess I am in a kind of mourning. Or doing penance. She's gone. History.

It is during this time that I encounter a big man with bangs and thick dark eyelashes. Six three, six four, over two hundred pounds. At a party, I notice him, the half-irony in his voice. I think, he's smart, mysterious. He tells jokes. He is handsome, strong, virile, and beautifully groomed.

"Singlehandedly, Julian Pendergrast can save this market, if he'll just get to work," H. J. whispers to me, over by the crawfish and tasso canapés. "That man is cachet walking. He knows houses are emotional—he understands," he says, misting. When I introduce myself, Julian says he's heard a lot about me. Then, leaning down—I'm not very tall—he goes on, "You look after Jessica, she's a Pandora, hunh cher?" I guess he is drinking vodka that night, but I feel like I've had an audience with the pope.

Julian still has his sense of humor during this period, the end of 1987, the beginning of 1988. These days while Jessica is gone, are the last ones like that. Sometimes I think of them now as innocent, carefree, the glory days gone by, but I shouldn't, I know.

"Beryl, honey?" I fill with tears. It's April.

She is out in Santa Barbara. She'll be back in a week. "Is that Botero still on the market?" she says.

Of course. The market is still dead in the water.

We have a great reunion lunch. Pegue's. But the concrete

yard is shabbier—moss has grown over most of the figurines. The food is even better, though. We eat outside under a creaky trellis. Slate slabs beneath our feet. She's done a pilot for a sitcom. Horrible, she tells me. Enough said. There is not a word of apology about that day she stood me up, and although that crosses my mind, I don't want to seem the kind of woman who cares. I want to be bigger than that. Jessica inspires me.

She asks me a lot about Julian and Mary Ann, his wife— they have two kids I say, and her eyes get really big again.

"Mary Ann still? Two kids? I thought just one."

I say he is doing all kinds of beautiful things out at Camellia Hill. Total historical accuracy. He's brought in a designer, and also the last great faux bois man in North America, to paint the cypress back the way it used to be, the way the English liked it, fixed up to look like maple, or cherry.

"I've decided to buy the Botero, and by the way," she says, her tongue between her teeth, "I'm getting married."

My spoon just drops into my smoked turtle and artichoke soup.

"Have you heard of Stanton Lymon?" she asks. "From New Orleans?" This last word, she pronounces "nu-rol-lins"—

Of course I know who Stanton Lymon is—one of those

Mind of the South types. Sometimes he comes on TV to explain what Creoles are, what Louisiana really believed during the Civil War, who shot Long—nobody ever seems to remember these things for sure. All the big questions are still left open, I've noticed, in Louisiana—are women people, did Elvis die, was slavery wrong? People here are still ready to argue these points. Stanton was apologetic, proud, and burdened, all at once. Fiftyish. A minor native celebrity.

"Don't you think he's cute?" she asks me. "I think he is sooo cute."

Out of the blue is not even the word. But I am the very first to know her wedding plans. This is a boost.

Settlement takes a while—Jessica is flighty, keeps changing things. She is paying the asking price, so I can't complain. We go to it one morning in March, 1987, I think. Stanton is there—he hasn't moved in with her, and they haven't wed as yet. He is still down at Tulane. The word is, after this last year, he's retiring early to St. Sebastianville, to write of course, in that fancy house with his tempestuous gorgeous wife and her Hollywood children.

Jessica's late. She doesn't wear black to the lawyer's office. She wears salmon, linen, I think, pleated, practically to her ankles—dramatic, but not in au courant style, in St. Sebastianville rich lady style, which is not at all the same. He is a little chilly, when we get around to signing documents. I figure he doesn't have to pretend.

We all know whose money it is.

After, Jessica starts two big projects at once—fixing up the Botero, and of course, the wedding. And I am involved in both. Especially the "Big South theatre," which is what she says she wants the reception to be. She wants all the elements—an oak alley, men crossing the lawn with tumblers full of bourbon, all the women wearing hats, lawyers with wide suspenders, Spanish moss, children dressed in batiste and ribbons.

These are still very dispiriting times. In June I ask H. J. what he thinks some grand home we are listing should be reduced to, and he says, "You take a stab," while he stares out the window upon the businesses in our strip mall that are finito, boarded up. The refurbishing of Camellia Hill is going too slowly, even. When sometimes I drive by it on my way to show a turkey, I notice it's wrapped in scaffolding, two tired-looking workmen at the very top, scraping a hundred and thirty years of paint off a Corinthian column, Julian out there, with that designer he's brought in, Xavier something—I don't know his name then—gruffly suggesting things to the help.

Not a lot of umph anywhere.

At the places I have to show, vacant now for years, I am beginning to notice the unkempt landscaping, cracked concrete, leaks down behind the sheetrock. There's nothing abstract about depreciation in places like this, where it rains sixty inches a year. After the Love River rises and houses I've shown at that end of town start to appear on TV with row boats tied to the hollow columns by the front door, the family on the roof, the dog barking at the TV news helicopter, I start to doubt my whole profession. "Flood insurance," H. J. says. "I swear, Beryl, they all have it. At least they'll get some money for their places. They are the lucky ones."

It is an escape, what can I say, spending time thinking about caterers. Julian's restaurant has the best chefs between the Love River and New Orleans. When I say this to Jessica, she seems to have a lot of trepidation. "Can you call him for me?"

I do. Of course they have to get together, whatever their past. I ask him to meet us where Jessie has suggested, on "neutral ground"—her term—at a coffee and beignet place.

When he walks up she bites her lips, even trembles. This is affecting. It is really a shame, I have to think, she hasn't made more movies. When he comes to the table her hand folds into his big square palm. Next to him she looks tiny, like a toy. "Well, Julian, I'm back where I started, baby."

"How it is?" he says softly.

"Maybe you can tell me," she says, losing her voice on the word "me." As if she intends no one else in the world to hear. You can feel it, something swirling around them, not love, exactly, more intense. I'm not sure what it is.

Eventually she tells me how she and Julian used to talk, all the time, in high school. He talked her into losing twenty pounds one summer, right in this same coffee place. When she did, he made the appointment, drove her down to the modeling agency in New Orleans himself. They made her original video. When she first went out to L. A., he came. He advised, explained, counseled and covered for her. He got her through doors, pretended to be her agent, press secretary, bodyguard, dresser, anything. When she started living with the producer, things went sour. They hadn't spoken in eight years, up until this day I got them together.

For the next two hours they carry on as if I'm not there, but occasionally they look over to check on me.

Mostly because of being engaged to Stanton, I think, and buying on the lake, she is popular with the rich doctors and lawyers now, those who are masters of their world, who don't care about Hollywood, only about themselves. "I really love them all," Jessie tells me over one of our lunches. "They all know exactly *what they want.* I don't even think they want what they can't have. Can you figure that?" She is wearing circle pins at her neck and driving a Volvo with the local private academy stickers on the back. She talks about what the rich crowd has settled for when they settled down. Which lawyers really wanted to be jazz pianists, but now they are rich so they don't care, which wives have mysterious illnesses, which ones are bound to lose their husbands and are exquisitely resigned to it, which fathers push their boys too hard at soccer games. She says to me once, "I think they all have had just enough luck. Never too much. They are so solid. It must be because they wake up in those beautiful houses. You think?"

These folks give Jessie and Stanton an engagement party in the early fall. I love this.

"Ready or not?" Randall asks me before we go out to it. Am I ready for a baby, he means. I am very surprised he has asked. I'm dumbfounded. It's been years since we have talked about this. It doesn't seem relevant.

That same night I meet Xavier Storm, Julian's New York designer. He's strange, a beady Zorro sort of figure.

Beaming, her face so young and fresh, her eyes widening the way they do, Jessica comes running up halfway through.

"He's going to let us." She is holding my hands, jumping up and down—she is light, the pressure is minimal. Ethereal, one critic has said.

"What?" I say.

"Julian's not only going to cater, he's going to let me have the wedding at Camellia Hill! He says he'll have enough of it finished." Jessica kisses me on both cheeks.

Xavier, who is standing there, says, "Isn't that going to mean a lot of people tramping through the house? What about the landscaping?"

"How do you know when she means it?" Randall says when she runs off to tell somebody else. He hasn't seen much of Jessica before. "Isn't she acting?" Somehow he is standing right there. I hadn't even seen him. Randall, I'm talking about.

"Did you hear about that voodoo doll?" Xavier says, his thin eyebrows rising. This man has a pencil mustache. "On her ex-lover's porch?" A pencil mustache, did you hear me.

"Oh, please," I say. Then I blurt this out, when I have no real way of knowing: "You are just jealous." I don't mean it the way it sounds. I haven't the foggiest.

Because of Xavier's and Julian's renovations, the wedding is put off twice. It almost rains on the day it finally happens in March but then the blue blasts in about one thirty—the ceremony is minimal, under a lovely striped awning. There's a grand buffet on six tables: prime rib and étouffées and crab and tasso and crawfish puffs and pies, a big cake brought up from New Orleans. On some tables there's mixed grill, others, gazpachos and gumbos, on others, just flans and fruit sauces and inventive little nouvelle raviolis. Jessica wears a waltz-length gown, silvery gray, beaded, an incredibly lavish hat two milliners in an ancient shop downtown spent weeks on. Black ladies. A work of art.

My own wedding was plain and cheap. We went to the caterer, we took the chicken plate. I gritted my teeth. But this is a perfect afternoon. And I really have arrived in this town. There's this grandeur, I know it. And we are all being watched: everywhere there are arty-looking men with dark shirts, baggy pants and skinny ties and big cameras. H. J. is out there on his third bourbon, pumping all the out-of-towners' hands, telling them the lore about marvelous St. Sebastianville, Louisiana, the whole history of families and fortunes long gone and furniture and houses and people who lost their bearings over all of it. There are a few stars there too. You'd recognize their names. But I'm not into that now.

Everybody looks beautiful. But the Hill is ravishing. The grounds were planted so long ago the camellia bushes around it are tall as trees, reaching to the bottoms of the second-story windows. The lawn is a huge pool of lipstick pink petals, unearthly. Julian is going for state of the art. He shows us the brick first floor, stripped back to the original, the kitchen, keeping room, bedrooms, the second floor, where the masters lived. Only about four of the rooms, out of eighteen in the main house, are actually complete, but nobody minds.

Xavier is still in the process of matching the scraps of ancient wallpaper, finding the right middle-Victorian furniture. They are scraping, stencilling. "Camellia Hill, Once Halcyon," is the title on the handouts we pick up in the foyer, which give a little history. The first owner, Hermes Bourgeois, took up with a slave named Zoe. He promised her the moon—he freed her, sent her down to New Orleans, set her up in business. But there was some tragic secret. No one knows. Perhaps he was really her father. In the end, he committed suicide.

"Oh, local color," Xavier turns, and remarks to me, "why don't you all go blind looking at it?"

I decide then and there he wasn't born Xavier.

Mary Ann, Julian's wife, smiles that whole day, shyly proud. She is enormous, nine months exactly—her third—with this interesting face—a wide jaw, a square mouth that has a slight uncertainty about it, something vulnerable and brave. She looks at you as if she doesn't want you to look at her so long.

While Randall is out in the back, grilling a legislator about a Superfund cleanup, I find Julian and Jessie alone. She is sitting on the counter, her dress up so high I can see her blue garter. He grabs her sleeve. He whispers in her ear. This isn't sexy exactly, it is complicated. I can tell you there are many their fun is at the expense of. I can practically see the subjects dropping like flies—the entire upper middle class of St. Sebastianville, all those ladies who told me those unkind things when Jessica first came back, and the ones who embraced her when she returned and bought on the lake, all those thick lawyers with the wide suspenders, the heavy shoes, who take only football seriously, consider politics entertainment, who threw the party for her, the same ones she was fascinated with two months ago. The solid people. The wedding guests. It's mean. They cannot stop, Julian and Jessie. They must go on and on.

These are the only things that day that make me feel even the slightest bit uneasy: how they are with one another, and Xavier when he comes up behind me, saying, "Julian likes *some women* so much, you know she was entirely his idea?"

When I'm a little drunker, though, I want to love everybody that day. I want to go home with Randall and tear his shirt off when it is over. I want to have twins at least, and dress them in linen edged with cutwork, and plant lilies all over the lawn, not to mention camellias. I start talking about making the back bedroom a nursery—adding ceiling fans, squares of crochet lace. Randall thinks it is just that it is spring and we are drunk and phenomenally well fed, but it is more, it is Jessica, it is Camellia Hill, it is how grand and beautiful and famous and still possibly mine this place feels.

Mary Ann Pendergrast has her third baby, a little girl, that night, and that is perfect, I think.

For about a month I am so high I'm sure I'll never come down. We try. I mean, Randall and I. For the first time, really. We try.

Jessie and Stanton are on a month-long trip to Spain.

During this time, something shows up in *People*. Now I think of it as a sign. I expect Jessica to be on the cover—really—and instead it's a piece near the back, one of those where-the-has-been-is-now articles. One photo: Stanton with his nice Gregory Peck slightly gray hair, Jessie in her magnificent hat, her beaded dress, her two children, hard to recognize without their Walkmans. The caption, *It's a fairy tale.* But this seems snide, the way they only print a tiny black-and-white.

\*   \*   \*

The next thing: Julian leaves Mary Ann for Xavier Storm. The new couple runs away to St. Kitts.

I am the most surprised person in St. Sebastianville. All H. J. has to tell me is "C'est la vie." I don't know Mary Ann that well. I am furious with Julian and I like him so much at the same time. I really don't know who to like, who to think is silly, who tortured, who is having an affair, what to wear, whether this is a wonderful or terrible place to live. I am a mess, really.

When Jessica finally comes back she tells me she's always known. She wasn't surprised when he married Mary Ann anyway. "We all knew. Mary Ann knew. But married men can be gay here, it's okay. He was better than the average. He wasn't like those other jokers on the lake. He wasn't so weighted down, so flattened out by being a man, or God save us, a southern man, like Stanton," she says, her eyes getting large again.

I am afraid to ask about Stanton. I can't take any more right then. "Not that I don't like men, but you have to understand, men are a different species down here, regular men. They are all like H. J. Birney—they carry the Southern man's burden, they have a desire for the end and the woods. And women get to be houses and town and wisdom and every pretty thing. And holding on and keeping steady. You know all this, Beryl?" She looks at me a minute too long. Everything she says, I think, is true. I am eating this up. She's wise, really.

This is what I am thinking.

"My Stanton writes this bull, that's okay, but I come to find out he believes in it!" she says. "Isn't it the most ridiculous stuff you have ever heard? Isn't it absolutely phenomenal? Is this 1988? Can't we drive a stake through Faulkner's heart?"

I'm just standing there, trying to figure out how any of this bears on Julian's behavior. He just had a baby!

"Maybe you'll catch on," she says. And I think, but how can that be? Through everything I am the one she tells things to. Look at me now: I am still a houseful of all Jessica Broussard ever told me. Ask me a question. I don't even want to know the answers anymore.

"Listen, Beryl, get it," she says, her eyes like raisins, like a weasel's, all of a sudden. "This whole fucking place is one gigantic motif."

I have no idea what she is talking about, really. She sounds crazy to me.

During this phase when Julian is on St. Kitts, Jessica is having bashes on the lake. Randall and I are "in." People are seeking me out as an agent. I know my way around those mansions. Then, that summer, Jessie paints the house buff, adds a wing. That fall she abruptly stops having parties and paints the place again, watermelon pink.

That winter, she does the kitchen over and then almost immediately she does it again. The first time she did the floor, she used what was popular—Mexican tile. Then she says to me once, offhandedly, around Christmas, "That floor has no give, glasses shatter when you throw them at people."

I don't ask.

We go out occasionally, and she describes the major moves—a study for Stanton, a room the kids can retreat to, so they can be out of his hair. "Don't get me wrong—" she says, correcting herself. "It is divine. Being married is divine." The widening eyes again. I can look right inside this time. Foggy, choppy seas. I can fall right through. I am even scared. I don't know how to take her lately. But still I am loyal. That's the trouble. I am so loyal to that woman.

When Julian and Xavier come back, they take up full-time residence at Camellia Hill. I hear they are completing the second floor. That fall and winter Julian visits with Mary Ann and the children, and of course the baby—his older son is eleven, his other daughter, six. They are civilized, even affectionate, it seems. I see them driving home from the Episcopal Church.

\*   \*   \*

Exactly a year after the wedding Jessica tells me she is tired, sick to death. We are at our old dive. Pegue has spruced it up, hired a restaurant consultant, hauled away the statuary—but the food isn't as good. Lingering over rubbery oysters casino, Jessica says, "They still won't let me be a person. They say I'm a mystery. I'm their Ava Garbo. They want to prove I'm crazy or a failure or a fake or put me in some other category—a nouveau riche, a hasbeen. I chose this. I did. Don't you believe me? I have scripts at home. They still send them. I could work again. You want to see?" She insists I follow her to her house to look.

It is true. People still talk. It is also true she has a pile of screenplays bound with plastic rings the way they do it in the copy shop, neat and modest—piled on an ottoman in one of her living rooms. I don't know how old they are. "You think you should blame a person for the kind of liver they have?" she asks me.

"Huh?" I say.

"I've never been able to hold anything—pills, anything. You need a good liver to make it out there."

She goes on to tell me more than I ever wanted to hear about stars and drugs and much worse in Los Angeles. She loves doing this. I can hardly bear to hear her. Depravity. True perversions. One on top of another. I get sick, just hearing. Why is she doing this? She only picks the movie stars I like. Finally, two hours have passed. She says, "Never tell anybody this stuff." I never will. Am I telling you right now? Maybe I should. Maybe everybody should. You listen to the rest of this, you tell me what you think.

Then she stares off for a while, before she comes up with the following. "I think I want to put the place on the market."

"Why?" I say.

"Stanton's going back to Nurollins."

"Oh, I'm so sorry."

"I'm not," she says. "Why should you be?"

That is a dagger. She means I'll make a sale. She is dealing in dirt, this day. And all the time I'm crying inside, all she's told me, and Jessica is breaking up with her husband.

"Listen," she says. She's aware she's hurt me.

Slow to catch on, I know what you are thinking.

"You want to surface again. You begin to think normal life would put you back in touch. You know what I mean? How many years have I been finding or fixing up a place to live in this town?"

"I've known you four years," I say.

"And I still can't get it right. Am I supposed to go back to L. A.? Am I supposed to go back there and try out for Ellen

Barkin's parts? Am I supposed to yack yack yack every week on some stupid show? Sitcoms are like perpetual summer camp, except you hate everybody, and the counselors hate you. I didn't like summer camp. I got heartsick. I was the first to crack. I was. Really. Every lousy show you see, the stars are all dreaming of eating each other alive. It's not a good life. Nobody believes me! Even Stanton doesn't get it, and he's an intellectual. He just takes me for some prize, for some grandiose prize, like I quit it all for him. I know what they say when I'm not there."

"Maybe they don't think what you—" I start.

"Oh yes they do," Jessica says. "I've known these people my whole life. Don't you defend them."

Her despair. It lands right in my heart. It goes off like a bomb. Nothing has ever made me feel as thoroughly sad.

Stanton doesn't go quietly.

For about eight months Jessica makes appointments with me and I make appointments with homeowners, and then she cancels.

There are stories. Screaming fights on that fancy lawn. The children dragging him in from the car. Her mother trying to patch it all up.

All of that, and I am still perfectly willing to put up with anything from Jessica that year. Randall wants to know why.

I haven't done anything to our house. I haven't gone to the specialist. I mean the fertility guy. I just can't make the call, face it. We aren't getting pregnant. "Oh, Beryl, this is so difficult"—that is about all I can get from Jessica, in a way of any apology. I am so so sad about her situation.

Then she vacates the Botero, takes the kids out of school, and puts her furniture in storage. Doesn't say where she is going. She sends me a card from London. She hires a tutor for the children. She is still thinking she might come back to St. Sebastianville someday. Keep me in mind, she says. "I want a real house."

H. J. comes in one morning, anxious with the news, gleeful. "Camellia Hill's on the market! Julian's losing his restaurant, too! He's overextended!" He turns to me. " Listen, Beryl. We don't want this place to get into the wrong hands."

I write her at her hotel in England, tell her the news. I am not thinking anything. Five days later she is back.

She has to see it. Camellia Hill.

I have qualms about this. I mean, she's a difficult client. She's dragged me through a lot. I feel butterflies, and this stoic sense at the same time, an I've-been-through-so-much-nothing-would-surprise-me attitude. I feel very southern when I notice this about myself.

\*   \*   \*

*"When are you going to deal with this, Beryl?"* Randall, when I go out the door, that morning—he wants us to go together to the doctor. I've decided I should, but I haven't. Something's not right. I'm in that unsteady territory you find sometimes in dreams.

Jessica is staying at her mother's little house—I've never been inside before. It is modest, in a sad little part of town. When I walk in, I see the back of the TV. I think Jessica is watching a show, at first, but she isn't, she is staring at the photos of herself propped up all over the top of the set. Her face *was* babyish in high school. It would have taken imagination to see she was going to be a beauty. She looked, well, with that big head, sort of dwarfish. There are the early magazine covers, her modeling jobs, and later shots I recognize— Perry, her producer, and Jessica half-squatting on the cover of *Vanity Fair*. "That's me," she says. "Me. I never exactly got that that was me. Do you get that?" she asks me. *"When it's you, I mean?"*

"I guess not, it never has been me," I say, that old wonder rising up in me, at what it must be like.

The children are standing there in their London togs. They are junior high age now, the girl has a skirt so short it is obscene, the boy has those English shoes with the soles.

He seems a little angry at everything. She looks over at them, as if they are strangers. The way they scowl, I decide maybe I don't want a baby. I decide to take back what I said to Randall that morning. This is what kids turn into. It is hopeless, anyway—I am getting up there. And marriage isn't something to count on.

Look at Jessie.

To show Julian's place, I've borrowed H. J.'s car. I've dressed up a little. That was H. J.'s idea. I've never, as an agent, shown a real plantation before, only all the fakes. But I am ready. I have the lore. Driving out there, I start to get excited. I have that whole house in my mind, in its completed, spectacular form. I know the blueprints. I have visualized. I have sat down with Julian, gone over the estimates. He has great ideas. He doesn't seem flattened or wounded to me. He still seems extraordinary as ever. I think of him as the most visionary native in St. Sebastianville. From him, I've learned so much about that house, its woods, its dates, its textures, its craft, who made the plaster medallions, under what conditions the cistern under the porch once worked. And how they were enhancing it. They were ambitious. I love knowing all this. I love walking around with a perfect Camellia Hill in my imagination.

Jessie is this tentative mess. She looks like a child, in something from a thrift shop, not old enough to be antique, cotton thin as a handkerchief. If I had put my fingers behind
the short pleated sleeves I think I could have poked them
right through. In fact, there are a few holes. She looks cos-
tumed for a high school play. But I have already overlooked
so much about her. I guess I am under a spell. That's what
Randall says lately.

Julian isn't living there—can't pay the bills. There's no
running water. I bring hot tea in a big thermos. I've tried
to think of everything—moist towelettes, tape measure, the
blueprints and estimates to finish.

When she gets in H. J.'s car she fondles the leather, as if
she's never been inside a Jaguar before. With this eerie smile
on her face, she asks me if the sun roof works. When it does,
when the wind comes in, she lets her huge head fall back,
whispers right in my ear so it tickles, these are her words:
"Okay, Beryl, I'm dying, take me." Then she giggles.

For the longest time, after we get there, she just wants to
stand at the end of the alley and take it in. I can't get her to
budge.

When we finally go inside, we spend a lot of time in Xavier and Julian's bedroom. She fondles the mosquito netting,
asks a lot of questions. I find this unkind—I'm separating

from Jessica, I think. I know this is the real thing. We talk camellias, crepe myrtles, we talk about the oak alley—getting the Spanish moss to come back. We talk about what she will do: a garçonnière for her son, music rooms, screening rooms, swimming pools, gazebos, topiary. I'm doing well. I can spot the real cypress a mile away, tell exactly how old it is by the color. I explain to her you can date the different additions to the house by the nails, the height of the ceilings—all the things the people in the really old families in town were apparently born knowing. She says, "You know so much, Beryl." But then she says, "You take a course?"

I laugh. It is a joke, isn't it?

Then, when I am done, she says, "Of course, I'll buy it. Why didn't Julian stay here so I could tell him?"

"He can't keep up the utilities."

"Oh, let me see the bills," she says rather businesslike. "Give me the truth."

She grills me for an hour, asks me about every figure. I'd never seen that side of her before. She knows what a dollar is. She really surprises me.

At first, selling Camellia Hill for three quarters of a million dollars isn't much fun somehow. It's crass, material. I think it is this being rich stuff coming between us. We are facing the real thing. We have to have our costumes all laced up.

Perhaps we both know this will be the end, or the beginning of the end. I am finally performing the service she asked me to do in the first place. I'm selling her the right house. Closure, here, no? I decide that's it, when I drive back to the office. It's been an incredible day.

H. J. goes wild. Champagne corks popping all over. I'm not sure where I stand. Things are not solid. They seem dreamlike. I am even going to be rich.

Julian has gone down to Cozumel, "to patch things up with Xavier." Mary Ann tells me this when I reach her with the news. She has a lot of equanimity, I think, for someone in her position.

Late that night I get a phone call directly from him. "Jessica's buying Camellia Hill? Jessica?" he says, so giddy. "You can't believe what this means, it's so, what can I say—" the line is very crackly "—resonant." Then there is a long pause. "Does she like the plans? The second garden? Not too much bath? Xavier's a fool for baths."

"She's going to do everything you set out to do, plus fix up the garçonnière for Sebastian."

"I've prayed for this. I've lit candles. I talked to the Black Virgin, I did. She talked right back. I thought it was just that I was drunk, oh, Beryl I just love you. I do. I'm going to come right home. I'm going to kiss your little head."

I can't sleep all night. I've had trepidations, but now I let go. It's beyond money again. I've found the perfect person for the perfect house. Everybody thinks so. Real estate in its sublime form.

But Julian doesn't come home quickly the way he said. He goes on to Xelha. Tulum. I get postcards of scrub jungles. Mayan ruins. They stay in Cobá, in a Club Med. I can't pin him down on a date for the settlement. Can't reach him that much. Maybe I don't try hard enough. Maybe I don't really want things to end. He's adopted me as a confidant. He writes, "We are sorting things out. It's wonderful. I pray every day."

But then he writes in a card later in the week, *I've never told the truth, you know that darling*—I think this was from Blanche Dubois, a direct quote, *I always tell what ought to be the truth.*

Nothing from Jessica all that time. She is still staying at her mother's. She can't get out of the house. She says she's under the weather. Then one day exactly a month after we signed the contract, she shows up at the office in an outfit I really can't fathom. The circle pin. The prim blouse, but this tight short skirt, slip-on shoes with elastic, bright green, as if she has dressed in the dark. Her hair is two colors, I'm not kidding. "You have to get me out of it," she says. "If I go to Camellia Hill then I'm nowhere. I'm out in the country. I'm not in with people."

I come up with the cliche of H. J.'s—we say this about all the mansions and the ugly spreads on the river now that the market had started to pep up. "Fifteen minutes and you are—"

"Downtown, I know, but that's not it, there's something about living there—"

"What?"

"I can't bring myself. At the Botero I kept changing the walls and the rooms and the floors. It was so I could at least still see them. So I could remember they were mine. Don't you get what I'm saying? I've had everything I ever dreamed since that day Julian drove me down to New Orleans." She squishes her chin so her lips are an open, distorted kiss. She doesn't look pretty. She is trying not to. "Just because of this. Does that seem real to you?"

She makes this sound like an affliction.

I feel the emotion. I am trying for the logic.

"Cross the river," I say, not knowing what to say, "and you're—"

"I'm downtown, I know, but don't I get to be a person?

Everybody else gets to! Don't you understand?" She pauses, then she says, "I've been trying to tell you this."

"What about Julian?"

"Julian got me into this mess!"

A vision comes to me, I don't even want it to—the trouble with Jessica's life: we are running through a hundred rooms, grand rooms with carpets, brocade, puddled drapes, Camellia Hill, then the Botero, ten movie sets, the wild walls falling away, tracking shots, zooming farther and farther out, that suburban hole in Bayou Arms, china at the dining table set for twelve, then her mother's little place with the ancient wooden blinds, the tired linoleum, the metal kitchen table, the little altar of her photographs, and opening the last door, finding no ground beneath our feet, finding only choppy seas, blue night, nothing. I feel scared. I want Randall. This is a sign, I suppose. I hold Jessica. This is Jessica Broussard, the movie star, I tell myself, she is real, real, real, realer than real, choking with tears in my arms.

"Find a clause," she says. "This is life or death. That place will be my tomb."

It is out of some mistaken belief in my honor, or out of my desire to have a stake in her, that I do this to myself and to

Julian. It's no advantage to me, on the face of it. It's dumb. Even as I'm doing it, this little voice is saying, no, no, no, you are foolish. But I do it anyway. Jessica was just more to me than me. That's my analysis now.

A clause. A clause. In Washington, we used the inspection clause.

"Down here, we don't encourage inspections," H. J. told me years before. "We can't be kept that honest. The ground is just too shaky, honey. We'd never sell anything. Don't tell them about the floodplain map whatever you do. It's up at the court—scratch that, I'm not even going to tell you where it is. Nobody would ever live in St. Sebastianville if they took a good look at the floodplain."

So I hire a guy I used to use, years ago, from Takoma Park. To get a little perspective on this situation. Anybody from New Orleans or St. Sebastianville might see things through a certain filter. It is an historic place. I tell the inspector to be "direct." I tell myself I can bear it.

We go back through Camellia Hill alone one very hot May day, just like the day Randall and I moved to St. Sebastianville—still, with the sky white. A whole new world opens up to me. The place is a wreck, an old crumbly house not built that well to begin with. Bug damage, half rotten. He pulls up boards and shows me things are completely undermined.

He takes a knife to the plaster friezes, which aren't even really plaster, but painted clumps of mud and Spanish moss and the hair of horses that died a hundred years ago. He gives me the estimate for a structural overhaul, not just the cosmetic renovation. It will take more than half again the price of the house. I already know the law—Napoleonic Code. If defects are concealed by the seller, there's really no sale. Contracts are null and void.

Jessica gets out of it. I lose a commission big enough to put me on the lake. H. J. is furious. "Why in hell did you do what she asked? Didn't I tell you she was crazy?"

"Then why doesn't anybody help her?" I say.

"She's a resource," H. J. says.

Randall is sort of relieved. He has been getting very nervous, figuring out ways to spend all the money I was going to make. He has been staying up nights, turning through catalogs, coming up with things to want. He confesses to me that he is getting tired. We are getting closer. I have started to cook.

Julian comes back sans Xavier. One night he calls me twelve times. "You can't do this, you can't," he tells me.

"It is in bad shape," I say. "It's my job."

"What about me?" he says. It is awful.

Next day he shows up on my doorstep. He's dark with his

Quintana Roo tan. Then, behind his glasses, his eyes are caves. He has a silver necklace, his tongue sticks to the roof of his mouth. He needs a lot of water. He's standing on my porch.

"Jessica Broussard should live in that house. That would be one thing I've done right in my life. I would gladly give it to her, I would. Tell her that."

"Would you like some coffee?" is all I can think to say. I have to let him come inside. Let him see my little place. We still don't have much. I can't decide how I want it to look.

"She's a legend," he says, trying to choose which piece of my pitiful furniture to sit upon. "People are starting to collect her in video. She's still beautiful. Did you see her in—" he fades in and out. Changes the subject. "That place is hers. The black virgin—Zoe . . . Let's rent *Palmetto*."

"She said it would put her too far away."

"Too far away? Too far away? She's light years away when she's in the same room. You know this."

"Maybe she's confused," I say. I am really surprised I let something like that slip. "Maybe she's not sure what she wants."

"Of course she does!" he says. "How can you even say that? You of all people, Beryl. I am so disappointed. It was for her, anyway. Everything I have ever done. Susan Hayward retired to a mansion in the South. She had a happy life, in the end, after all her trials. Do you remember her walk? Did you know one leg was shorter than the other, that gave her such a sensual walk?"

"Julian, how can you say that?" I say. "You're Julian Pendergrast, you do all these amazing things."

"I'm nothing," he says. "I'm not even alive compared to her. You are the same." Then he leans toward me, staring down my dress, and whispers, "Berylee, honey, Jessica c'est moi."

"That isn't true," I say. "She's herself. So are you yourself."

"Never," he says, back, snorting. "Never that. God. I hope not."

We are both sitting on the floor at that point. We cry. I've betrayed everybody. I've seen everything the wrong way. Even Randall, and also myself. I don't even know why. I'm just beginning to see the dimensions of this gigantic error. The horror.

Julian starts camping out in Camellia Hill. Sleeping out there on a pallet. Pills, bourbon. There are many circumstances, not just our backing out. I keep wanting to call him, tell him I know what the problem is, what we've got to do. But I don't call. His son is doing every kind of drug. Xavier has taken him to the cleaners. The debts are huge. Mary Ann has even told him to stay away—to go into a chemical dependency unit. One night, about six weeks after his last visit to me, he drives into River Road, doesn't look both ways.

There's a semi.

The same morning Julian's death is announced on the news, she comes to my house. I am surprised she knows where I live. "You made me do it," she says. "You made me!"

"Me?" I say.

"You always believed in me. In your idiot northern naive way. You, you thought I meant what I said. I tried to explain to you."

"What did I do exactly?"

"You!" she says.

"What did I do exactly?" I ask her again.

"You made me feel like I knew what I was doing."

"Now I know what you are doing, then," I say, growling. "What?"

"You are leaving," I tell her. I can't believe it is me talking. "You are leaving."

She goes. Out of my life. Almost. I feel like I will fall apart the next minute. I feel dismembered. When I slam the door in her face, my one nice thing—an Audubon quarto print—falls off the wall. That is about right. Did I mention to you all the birds Audubon painted were dead? He shot them first. Here, in south Louisiana. To get that lifelike detail. A guy in the Sierra Club told Randall this.

Of course, people are saying Julian's death, his ruin, are her fault. This is all over St. Sebastianville.

Call me a masochist—I think I'm just confused. I feel like an accessory. I come up to her at the funeral—she just stares right into me, not a word at first. She is wearing a black lace scarf. She looks, well, out of a Velázquez. What is it like to have a face like that, I hear myself think. With a face like that your life is larger than life. Your life is so big other people can actually almost parse it out, decipher it, whereas mine is too small to get even a good look at. I notice these feelings, for what they are, for the first time, really, that day. I am appalled by myself. Utterly appalled.

But I am standing right next to her anyway.

"Don't listen to them," I say, *entre nous*. I half know this is stupid. I know I am being romantic. I know these are old habits of mind. "Nobody here knows anything."

"Well, that's kind of you," she says.

"No, no," I say, "it's perfectly true. None of them deserve you, none of them. They all have nothing lives."

"No," she says again, "I mean it's kind of *you*, Beryl."

The worst part is, there is a way she is right.

When we are lowering Julian into the ground, I decide I have to leave St. Sebastianville. It is who I am here, the falseness I believe. I have said too many yeses. I don't even exist. Randall and I have a huge fight that afternoon. I tell him to just take me away. He says, "For the longest time, I was dying to leave. But now I like it. I'm getting things done."

I say, "There's only less pollution because all the industry is dying."

"That's not true! Don't change the subject! Why can't we try harder?"

I say, "It must be the pollution or the way we don't fit in—"

"Why haven't we bought a couch yet? Why didn't we put up some curtains?" he asks, tromping through the house.

I don't know the answer. "Why don't we move somewhere that makes sense?" I say. "This place is crazy."

"Like?"

"Vermont."

"Candyland?"

"I hate it here," I say. "Why are you taking its side?"

"There's no antidote," he tells me. "This is our life, Beryl. This is where we live."

No one has ever said anything more painful to my ears. I can't speak to him for days.

The bank is fed up with us real estate types, decides to sell Camellia themselves as is—no warranties, no guarantees. All defects unconcealed. H. J. comes in to tell me, defeated, "They are dumping it, the bastards." The word is Jessica has decided to make a big bid. She is all set up to attend the auction—she has researched the title, all the liens. I haven't helped her. She and I aren't speaking.

"Well, I want it," H. J. says to me before he goes. "Of course I want it. I want to keep it in the right hands."

"You said three months ago Jessica had the perfect hands," I tell him.

"I love that place so much I can taste it," he tells me. "I'm going to develop that whole side of the river." He shows me plans. Plans are cheap, but I don't know this.

I go. I can't help myself. H. J. seems to have such lust. And Jessie wants the place desperately, more and more as

H. J. bids past her. It is over Julian, of course. She must feel terrible. She has feelings, I'm thinking.

The price gets over a million. "What are you going to do, H. J.," I say in the heat of things, "liquidate the whole company?" I mean his firm. The one I work for. He looks at me like I am crazy.

"What? It's a wreck. You had that guy from up north inspect it."

Jessica gets it for 1.5 and a dollar, about twice what she can really afford.

Actually, this will make her broke. We know it. H. J. and I have seen her financial statements. We've sold her two houses already. As soon as the gavel goes down, he's hauling out of there, his car radio blasting. He's bluffed.

I go into work the next day. I'm mad. "What do you believe in?" I ask him.

"Jessie will be happy now," he says. "She wanted trouble. She's got it. She suffered from an easy life."

"You know that's a lie. I know for a fact that's a lie," I said, although it was sort of true.

"Why waste faith on the facts?" he asks me. "Listen, Beryl: most people, if they had to take it straight on, would give it up. You believed in Jessie Broussard, flake that she is, for crying out loud. You take the cake."

"So what do you believe in?"

"I don't believe, I know, that St. Sebastianville, Louisiana, is the very core, the beating heart, of *Gracious southern living at affordable prices.*" He's reading off our brochure. He is in such a good mood. I decide he must be the devil.

He keeps going. He threatens me: "What's anything worth but what somebody says they'll pay? If you tell people the way it is, Beryl Jackson, that's deflation. This whole market comes crashing down, to dust. I *told* you this. That's my message. Learn from me. I saved us yesterday. We have million dollar homes now. We have movie stars retiring here."

I get the message: you must change your life.

First thing, I quit H. J. Birney Homes.


Now I sell houses for myself. I don't gossip. I try not to use any myths. I am very realistic with my clients. I say things like, "Have you thought of downscaling? Have you considered how many square feet you actually need? Do you think you will ever use the jacuzzi?"

These days there is new construction, people moving in. When I have clients who are from out of state, I have to show them the slab homes, the big old things on the lake have all been bought now. Even the turkeys are sold: people went in and tore out all the "galore" amenities, put in new ones, almost as awful. I tell my clients about the floodplain, suggest inspections.

I've been this way for some time now, and it works. Randall likes me better. When he talks about the past, he takes my side, he calls me an honest businesswoman. I was completely innocent, I mean, regarding Julian and Jessica. I was doing a job, a job, I was honorable, I worked against my own interests.

The great news: now, at thirty-eight, Randall and I are pregnant, I can hardly believe it, but it is so. My life has this tangible quality to it. We have furniture, people over. I have a reputation. I feel this different way, it's odd, content. When I'm with other people, I always remember I'm in the picture.

But a week ago I show a pretty house to a rich couple from New England. Their faces fall when I tell them the columns across the front don't really hold anything up. When I say the subdivision used to be a swamp, that's the reason it has so many lakes, they give me that we'll-let-you-know line. Then yesterday I hear they've gone over to H. J.'s people. He's my arch enemy now. So I'm down, but I feel like I'm coping.

And this morning: I run into Jessie going into the grocery store, her little legs poking out under some big top. She still wears those leggings which are a cliche now, the movie star sunglasses. Who she looks like is a nobody. And I have proof she's a bitch. You've heard it. We say hellos, anyhow. It's our history.

When she goes inside, I just come up with things. It's spontaneous, these speculations. Like, maybe she has a raison d'être now, fixing up that mansion the way Julian would have done it. She's scraping by, broke as all get out, struggling to keep up appearances. An old story. A tragic figure. A southern heroine. And Julian isn't really dead, he lives on, well, in a way he does. Maybe Jessica was Julian, after all, somehow. In a magical way. I think a lot of people tell her no these days, not yes. Maybe she really wanted that. I almost want to ask her. I mean, if I'd said no, wouldn't Julian still be here. Perhaps that was my mistake. I have to learn this lesson in life: everybody is real the same. Not some more real and some less. These things go through my mind.

I flash on that day I took her out to Camellia Hill. She is wearing that thrift shop cotton dress. The thing has tiny holes in it, that old voile you never see anymore, a little spray of baby's breath print, on a navy background. She is wearing a flat crushed blue straw hat. She is still rich, then, remember. Wealthiest client I ever had. When we get out of H. J.'s hunter green Jag, she tells me to come over and see. She is under one of those oaks, at the far end of the alley. We have a postcard view of the house, its eight Corinthian columns, porch, balconies. It is gorgeous. Painted buttercream and white. I say we can park closer—we are standing a quarter a mile away. She says, her eyes getting wider and wilder, "Let's look from here." We stand there together in the sweet heat for the longest time—

Now, with all my heart, I promise you, I speak from weariness here, from exhaustion, I pray someday that such dreams will leave this place, forever, and me, and mine, I do, I do, but I must confess:

That day that we went out to Camellia Hill and stood watching it glowing through the wavy, rising air, before we touched anything at all, before we took possession, before it yielded to us, before our feet tread on its old floors, before we added up its sums, before we knew its secrets, before we lost Julian—oh, please don't tell anybody this—

It was the happiest day of my life so far.

Don't say a word.

# DESIRE

If you ask me why I chose this life, I have an answer. It begins at a time in the city when there was no money for art.

A woman came up to me in a gallery. I knew her. "Marcus, is that you?" she said. "How long have you been in New Orleans?" This was almost one syllable, Norl'ns. She held the whole word in her mouth like a lozenge, no need to pronounce it at all, since there was only one place anybody could be talking about, why spit it out? A whole world came with that pronunciation—a beautiful, secret life. I felt a yearning that was fresh, like news.

She said to me, me, extending her hand, "I'm Vivian, Vivian Pollack? Remember me? Moreau, nowadays—" She was blonder and she was wearing expensive silk, bluish, like suede. When we were in college together in New England, she was said to be one of those girls it was nothing to have.

I hadn't had her. "Oh, Marcus Stone, this is my husband, Greg."

Greg wore wide, silly suspenders. He was broad-handed, fortyish, a big rock, opaque. Next to him she was a sylvan pond.

"We live over in the Garden District," she explained. This was their first time here, she went on. My gallery, a co-op, the St. Charles Art Center, was absolutely broke—we were soliciting donations that day. I was bad off myself—I had started thinking about selling my house.

"You'll have to join," I said, "become a patron."

She had been my model in the seventies, when I was sure I was destined to be a famous landscape photographer some-day. Once when my shoot was finished—she was nude, we were in the woods—I wrapped her up in a big old coat, and she said, "Oh Marcus, I love you," like that, so I wasn't sure what she meant, exactly, it didn't matter then. But that afternoon as I was standing there begging, I held onto the idea that she might have loved me once. I did so all along.

I called my friend Jerome that night, asked him to meet me at Mandina's, my favorite restaurant, to lift my spirits. As usual, he lumbered in late. He was a wiry, dark-eyed, generous guy. A cellist. The symphony had recently laid him off to save money—they were nearly bankrupt. Oil prices had collapsed. It was a depression in Louisiana, we agreed. But he seemed serene. In his spare time, he explained, he was going to classes at a meditation center on Magazine.

"This guy, the teacher, has a narrow face," he said, "you know, sort of Mitch Miller. Birkenstocks. He goes by Max." Jerome stroked his wide square jaw, as if to smooth the corners. "He said, 'Imagine all of this is being watched from Alpha Centauri.' Our junky hopes, our disappointments."

Wasn't Alpha Centauri some kind of car? No, it was a star—I was trying to concentrate, but instead I was thinking about easy white hips, round and perfect as twin moons. I only made pictures with her, with Vivian, never anything else. I had many women when I was in college—they came to me without my effort.

Maybe I didn't want to listen to Jerome because I'd heard most of this before. I'd already lost someone to Buddhism. San Francisco in the early eighties. Anna. We broke up over my horrible slump. I was not getting published, had no gallery. My failure was a huge gorilla that followed me from room to room. Anna came back from a retreat with her head shaved. She'd concluded I was too attached. "To what?" I said, because, for the life of me, I couldn't get attached, I thought that was the problem. The man's problem? Not being attached enough?

Much later I saw her on Van Ness Boulevard with two big Yodas, Thai monks, in brown robes, the kind who carry bowls. "I want you," I told her. I was stupid. "Now?" she said. My whole body was at this crest, this peak of wanting, unbearable, almost. "Now?" she said, again, saying no, very sweetly.

Her bumper sticker: *No Mind No Problem.*

Not long after that, I took a job in New Orleans, teaching at a private school. Four years later, in November, 1987, I was sitting in Mandina's with Jerome, having reached the great get-on-with-it age of thirty-five. Since September, I'd been put on half-time. Art had been reclassified by the directors as "enrichment." The waiter came by, offered to swish a little more sherry into our turtle soup. We slurped up the fabulous broth, went through two baskets of bread—no entree.

I don't think it was even a week later I got a call offering me work. Out of the blue. So, the gods were finally with me. I was blessed. A woman I knew who did video for lawyers said a movie company was looking for locations. She wouldn't say what kind of film. Would I just go out and shoot these streets? It was good money. I did half of Mid-City, Bywater. I took all the clichés—wooden jalousied balconies, haunting gates that led into courtyards. The houses

I loved, the ones collapsing, in ruin, the old Creole raised cottages.

Still, sending off the prints, one hot day around Christmas, I felt a fresh doubt. I'd done a lot with dancers and performers in the streets, architecture, and palms before, with no such feeling. It was New Orleans. Of course I took New Orleans pictures. But this time, there was some essence in the images, the way primitive people talk of it. For a second, I felt like a snatcher.

Then in January, the movie's art director, a woman named Sidney, came to town. She loved my pictures. Some money had come through, to actually make the thing, it was for real. Would I take her around and show her the locations?

I drove an ancient, cozy, problematic Saab then. When Sidney got in, she noticed the dash was real wood, as she felt across it for the ashtray's opening. Once she got her More cigarette lit, we were off down the Esplanade. "I love this city," she inhaled. "Oh, that looks like *Pretty Baby* . . . that's *Down By Law* . . . do we want *Death in Venice*? . . . That's not it, that's not the real New Orleeens . . . no, no, no . . . oh, slow down."

The way she said "LEEENS" bothered me. I tried to be agreeable, but I found myself taking the city's side, silently, deeply. Then, in front of one silly, watermelon-pink house, she started to breathe so I noticed, saying, "Stop, stop, I can't stand it." She was wearing a catsuit. Her jewelry, heavy as tools. Her hair, Ajax-washed. She told me, "This building satisfies me on every level."

By late in the day, it was clear. Even though I knew it would be good business to make an overture—maybe I could get to L. A., I could *change my life*—I couldn't bring myself.

At the end of our tour we were idling in front of her little bed-and-breakfast on Ursulines. "I haven't told you about the script," she said, lingering. "Come in. There's an honor bar."

I said I was famished. She reminded me we could eat. But I left anyway, and drove through the city, thinking about what was inside all the courtyard gates. It was true, when Vivian was easy I didn't want her. This just colored my desire with excruciating rue. When I got home, there was an invitation to a party at "The Moreaus" in my mail. And this was grand, this was wonderful.

Vivian's house was large, lavish, Uptown. The doors made me small, seedy. The ceilings were more than fifteen feet. The walls were cool greens or pinks, the moldings high up, heavy, curvy. "I didn't think you'd come," she told me as her arms slid back down from her quick touch on my shoulder, making a rustling sound. I got to smell her. Woodsy.

"There's a Mr. Hoffman here," she said, "who you can talk to about the St. Charles."

She handed me over to a short man in a strange brown suit who wanted to have a conversation about the photographs of Rosamond W. Purcell. Later I wandered towards the front parlor. Vivian was there, holding an iced tea tumbler full of gin and tonic, saying, "We're a pretty dull bunch up here, don't you think?"

I was about to answer, but then I noticed her nipples under her blouse.

It was the whole house I wanted. I wanted to steal it, and have her—this is what I felt, it was violent, it galloped up and down my trunk. "Are things okay? Did you mingle?" she said.

"I talked to Hoffman," I finally managed.

"His wife is the one who does things," she said, distracted. "And Greg and me, definitely. Don't count us out. Call on us."

For a moment she was looking in my eyes. I was sure of it.

On my way out, in the dining room, I discovered two dark hills of hand-dipped chocolates, tall as toddlers, on the wide mahogany table.

"Where is that college you and Vivian went to? New

Hampshire?" a Samantha in a stretchy crushed velvet dress said to me rather loudly. We'd been introduced. I'd already decided her hip bones would stab me. I was gobbling the chocolates. Belgian. The flavor was so intense I wished to be alone with them.

Then I caught Vivian in the mirror behind us. I recalled I had the negatives. I managed to get the fallen birches and the tone of her skin to have exactly the same silvery value, so she was almost imperceptible in the landscape. An egg. You had to search for her, seek her out, like animals in a tree trunk in a drawing in a book for children. I made her stay there, naked in the woods. It was cold, it wasn't even spring. I made her freeze.

"Can we have coffee sometime?" she turned and asked me.

"Sure, yes," I nodded.

"Maybe I can bring Samantha and we can go down to the gallery. She needs art, something, don't you think?" she whispered this last part.

Yes, yes. I left, exploding, hazelnut creams in my pockets.

Right after Mardi Gras, Jerome and I met again at Mandina's. Things were worse all around. I'd put my house on the market; he was working part-time at a music store. He was still sitting with Max. He started telling me how to meditate.

"You don't *watch* your breath, you allow it to happen."

But I knew how. I'd always been able to slow down until I could perceive the blood rising and rushing in and out of the veins in my head, darkening my field of vision, then brightening it again. Since I was a child, I had done this, spontaneously.

"Some doctrines teach that there is a world out there, outside of mind, others say it is all up here, every bit. That's the Mind Only school. Which do you think it is?" Jerome said. "I asked Max, I said, 'Doesn't the realization that form is emptiness and emptiness is form take the pleasure out of the world?' I'm an artist, see," Jerome hesitated, was I with him. " . . . I'm interested in beauty. If all form is empty, I mean, why make it at all? You know what he says?"

I said what.

"He said the emptiness makes things more beautiful, when you see them as they are."

I was afraid Jerome was going to continue to explain this, but that second our soft-shell crab po'boys arrived, dressed.

I think it was March when the movie people actually came to town. I saw it in the *Picayune*. A week before shooting started, Sidney called me. Would I be the still photographer. The second lead's boyfriend had the job, but he'd run off to New Guinea. This was a coup. This was a big deal. This could save me. It was a thousand a week. When she said it was about a modern voodoo queen, my heart sagged some, but I said, "Great."

It turned out to be horror, zombies, pseudo Cajuns, voracious ghosts. Sidney's assistants and the others, the assistant's assistants, the sound men, the grips, showed up every day dressed for a Haitian hoedown—jeans and straw hats, sandals. They bought put-a-spell-on-you oils from the tourist shops in the Quarter. They were too young. Their gullibility was spectacular, legendary—they roamed the city like scavengers, a handsome naive swarm. On the set, I ate with Sidney, who was more my age. I got used to her. Sometimes we hugged, kissed cheeks the movie people way. One day after I'd been photographing the female lead who, in the story, swallowed her daughter's soul to be immortal, Sidney said to me, "There's somebody, Marcus. You're obsessed." There was pain in her voice, I could feel it. It wasn't hers, though, it was as if she knew mine. I was crazy about her for a second.

But that night, I called Vivian. When she answered, her voice silky like water, I hung up.

By the end of April, after the shoot was over, I hadn't been paid completely. Rapidly, I was lowering the price on my house. Then, one day—I think it was the full moon—a couple from Boston took a quick look. Next thing you know, they offered cash. They were going to use it for vacations. "Like it was a bon bon, bam," the agent said. She was a Creole, lovely—her hair was pulled back like a ballet dancer's. She wasn't thrilled New Orleans had got so cheap people from other places bought it outright.

When I met Jerome that night for drinks, I said, "Pocket change to them." I laughed.

Touching our check just as I told him how broke I still was—I'd made no profit—Jerome said, "Move in with me," and a curtain opened. His sweet eyes grew larger, and I realized, even as I knew he had loved women.

He was abashed. He put his dark eyes away, somehow, without having to look down. "I didn't mean," he said, pausing. "Well, sort of I did."

It was awkward then, it was hard to keep talking.

That night, going home, I encountered pretty women leaving the restaurants where they worked. I'd seduced girls like these from the time I was a college boy. I was still a good-looking man—one would come with me, maybe two. But it was enough, more than enough, this night, to look at them in their white blouses and black skirts, running down Burgundy smoking too many cigarettes, calling out to each other about the tyranny of bosses. I thought of doing an essay about them, the way Brassai did his Secret Paris, but then, I thought, everything in New Orleans had been shot already. It was shot.

By summer, I really didn't own very much. My equipment, my CD player, my Saab, which was dying, my futon, my lamps. My vehicle was very light, as I might say now. I found a place in the Quarter with walls a pale terra-cotta. Very high old ceilings. Jerome didn't return my calls. He wrote in a note, a kind of apology, that he had been "turning over a lot of rocks" in meditation.

The St. Charles Art Center people called to say they could only pay the utilities through June. I was on the board. Could I get the money?

I called Vivian. I got her maid. I said nothing.

In May, Jerome finally got in touch to say the Cincinnati Chamber Orchestra had offered him a position, for terrible pay. We met for a farewell dinner. I wanted to tell him no, no, you are my only friend, stay, please, but he kept changing the subject. "Isn't this supposed to be a stereotype?" he said, laughing over crawfish and too much beer. We were at a place with tables outside, his idea. "The starving artist? Aren't stereotypes supposed to be false? What are we starving for?" he asked me, his voice rising in unusual places. Meditation had not helped him too much, I decided. Besides, we were very full, stuffed, in fact. "What?" he went on, and I didn't know, I didn't. "Beauty? Now what is that?"

So I went down to Magazine Street a couple of days later. I sat in the hall on a little pillow, with the class. Max noticed me. After a while, in the incense-scented darkness between breaths I conjured her light grey eyes, her ballet slippers, her round hips, her pearl earrings, and I was back there at her exaggerated house, gobbling chocolates, taking her upstairs, kissing her neck, her ears, watching her arch her back, watching her love every minute of it. It was Vivian or nothing. I was clear.

First of June, I got my money from the movie. I'd get through the summer. Then, on impulse, I wrote a huge check to the gallery. At the same time, I called her. When she answered I talked this time. I said, "Don't bring Samantha."

We met at the Café Du Monde, the huge open café at the river near Jackson Square, in the center of the Quarter. When I first lived in New Orleans I thought this place was for tourists. Then I realized the people were natives, not out-of-towners pretending to be continental by having café au lait and powdered sugared beignets and talking and talking, but people for whom going to a café is as natural as breathing, like people in France. The tourists stayed ten minutes, as if the Café of the World were a mess hall. The difference was, the natives lingered. They knew that much about pleasure.

She talked a little about some of her favorite restaurants in the neighborhood, and I realized I hardly ate anymore. I couldn't stand, for example, the scent of meat. I wondered if it was my poverty or my recent poverty of desire, or just the heat. I kept this secret. Like I kept it a secret about my pictures, how lately I had this feeling I was being a thief. How I believed I stole her once, how sorry I was, at the same time I wanted to steal her again, but who she was, this time, not her look.

"You know about the gallery?" she said, after a few minutes. "Did I tell you Greg's boss's wife is doing a big bash, down at the museum, see if we can do something about all this slump?"

"No, no, no. No no," I said. I was touching her arm. It was solid. It was not only in my head. This was wonderful news.

"Are you all right, Marcus?" she asked.

Touching her, I was aware of her skeleton. The Tibetan Buddhists save bones, someone was telling me down at Max's center. They make trumpets out of human femurs, punch lamas' skulls into beads, hang them about their necks, to remind themselves how transitory is existence. But they still cling to bones. They still cling. I have thought of this paradox since, many times.

"Tell you what," she said. "Let me see your work. I have this den, Greg says it is too dark."

I let her talk.

"I don't know many artists anymore," she said. "In fact, you were about the only one I knew then—you were so cool, so interesting—"

The Vietnamese waiter brought the coffee, the beignets. It was late afternoon. Vivian was wearing a shiny raincoat, underneath that a small, periwinkle blue dress, silk. In a few hours, she was going to the wedding of the son of one of her husband's clients. She said, "I spend a lot time doing things like this. It's a job, it is."

The evening singers and dancers were moving into the square. One man posed on a box, a waxen Cleopatra. There was an extraordinary mime, another man who ate fire all night long down in front of the Cabildo. I had taken all their pictures on other days. I have these even now. Only St. Germain des Prés in Paris is comparable on nights like this one. It is enchanted when they move in. She said, "I thought I might end up some other way, you know, but I never had a great imagination."

"Come walk over to my place, I'll show you," I said. I would put up her hair and kiss her neck, there, there where we sat if she didn't understand me. People kissed in the Café of the World. It happened all the time.

Her lips were less closed between words.

I slid my arm around her waist. We almost ran to my apartment. There the paint was peeling, but this time of day, not quite sunset, it was beautiful. I stood in the middle of my living room and showed her no prints.

She kept looking at me, and then she said, "I thought you wanted me to look at some to buy."

"Maybe that too," I said.

"Well," she said. "I guess, Greg."

"Greg?" Of course the weight of Greg was great, but I said the word lightly, I had to. By some conspiring magic, the word lost all its density as I said it. Sometimes this happens.

"He's always telling me I'm falling to pieces, I'm not as pretty, you know, got to have his cheerleader—that's the deal," she looked away. "So it didn't occur to me. You never seemed—" She had a deep breath, finally taking this in, what my staring at her meant. Then she asked, "Have you been calling and hanging up?"

I nodded yes, and she said, "I need this." No irony.

My futon was on the painted floor in the second room.

Some time later she sat at one end of it, her clothes a shimmering puddle beside her. And I was hovering over her small soft body, when I should have already started to make love to her. She started to say, "Does everything have a reason?"

There was pleasure everywhere I looked, her beige nipples, her narrow legs, the sunset light, low and vital, whirling, pinkish golden. I said, "How are you?"

"Why are you talking?" she said, her hips closer. "What is there to say say say?" she said.

Now this part, I couldn't help.

When you dive into a clear pond, it isn't the liquid eye in the land anymore, it turns into a series of cold prickly swirls around your arms, a dance of blood in your torso, the spider of a splash across your cheeks, the tentative, cloudy bottom under your feet, unsteady, the shiver of a fish passing you. There is the work of becoming accustomed to the water, which is nothing like the idea of a swim, really. Nothing like the pond you have known before the dive.

She was a pressure, a rich sensation, surrounding me, sounds, breath on my face, the scent of woods, tingling, sparkling, these explosions among my senses. It was extraordinary, ravishing.

But I couldn't get to Vivian the one I wanted.

I let go when I was done. When she was done. She went

into the dark little bath I had. Later, half-dressed in the doorway, she said, "I'll call you," looking around as if afraid she
could be seen from the street. "I'm not saying, 'I'll call you,'
I will, I will, really."

I think she didn't know what to do with my face, and the
quick nature of this hour had a strangle on us both. When
she left, her dress was slightly damp, yet it swayed. The way
her shoes clicked down my hall. That and the quick rustling.

I stood in that ending pink sunlight for some time after. I
was naked and this light was a great red crescendo, burning.

In the morning I went to Max's, and I stayed there twelve
hours. This was the day I set out upon the path.

Since, I have come to be grateful for my glimpses of reality, one of which was this night I've been speaking of, when
I was caused to question the content of ecstasy after this ex-
quisite woman left me alone, while the sun went down over
New Orleans.

That was long ago, but I can still see her coming out of
my bathroom, in her satin slip. I sense her curiosity at me. I
see the tinge of boredom in her eyes. As soon as she dressed
and started to go, she was more what I desired. This is true
of that whole city as I think of it now—its doorways, its
curves and scents, its food, Jerome's eyes, the coral lush of
the sunset light, the Café of the World, the girls who run

down Burgundy in black skirts, the fire eaters in front of the Cabildo. The farther I am from those days, the more marvelous their features, their shape, their meaning.

This is the conundrum of form, I think: when those days were mine, they were hollow.

Now they are brimming and gorgeous.

# THERE IS A RIVER IN NEW ORLEANS

That night Gerald asks me a riddle: what is a river, really, its waters or its old banks?

We are in a restaurant. One of the waiters comes up to tell him he has a call. He hesitates. It would be rude to leave. He's a gentleman. I once enjoyed that. My father liked him. My mother, too, in her way. Gerald used to be my husband.

"Go," I say, "I know you'll be right back," which softens his face. We have issues to talk about tonight, what will happen to our daughter—but all I can think about is my mother, who isn't even alive. The July sun hasn't set yet. With Gerald gone I can see out the restaurant window that the Mississippi is winding through the city of New Orleans. You never see it at street level here, because the levees are in the way.

The banks last.

She was a beautiful woman, people said of my mother. She was from a good family, French Huguenot, rare and dark-eyed, and she was given to singing at the wrong times—at the table, in front of the help. Where I grew up people said that if my mother had been someone less mad, my father would have been governor, or something close. My father was considered by others long-suffering. He was a lawyer, a long-legged man who wore his seersucker suits loose. He even had ideas about progress of a kind.

Her soul was a bird closed up in a drawer.

*Why do you sleep in daytime clothes,* Gerald used to ask me. He thought that was low, which meant, I thought then, while we were breaking up, that he was disappointed a girl raised by a good family in a house on a corner in a dreamy southern town had not been brought up a lady and wouldn't forever act like one. Antique as that sounds. I don't act like a lady now, no, not ever, all my old friends who used to tell me to live a little in college would be proud of me. But truth be told, I wasn't raised at all. I grew like a stalk.

She'd drive away, sometimes, without telling the maid or us where, and then we'd wait at the kitchen table. It would be me and my younger brother and my sister, my father off lawyering, the maid's ride—a friend of hers or an ex-husband with a car—would have come to get her at five-thirty, and be long gone. We'd wait while the butter on the cooked carrots cooled to tiny yellow puddles. I can smell that kitchen, see the high ceilings, the top pantry cabinets filled with Limoges we never used. The smell of spicy beef, cooked ketchup, the sound of onions snapping in grease, the meat loaf blackening in the oven.

I believed things would turn out, and my mother would, she would, come back. But I didn't tell anybody this. I'd insist we play cards, war or old maid, and entirely ignore the hour, the facts. I knew the world was beneficent when I was thirteen, that it was beautiful if you knew where to look. My daughter Juliana is thirteen now, and she knows the same.

I'm supposed to be gazing down at the artistic veal medallions with a Madeira sauce just set before me by another waiter, but I look up and see Gerald, across the room. He startles. I've caught him being alone. It's a bad habit he must want to conceal.

When I was twenty-eight, I felt ninety, gristly and old, all these memories would bubble out of my bones when he moved towards me. I never told him what I was thinking then.

She didn't believe things could ever get better, my mother. Or ever change.

After I divorced, her old sadness came and stayed with me

for its first long visit. It was unanticipated, this grief. After all, I had asked for the divorce. It visited me anyway, the sense of irretrievable ruin—my daughter's tears when she came home from kindergarten after Gerald moved out, her sleeplessness when she returned from one of her long stays with him, the open loss I saw when I faced my house's emptiness once he'd closed the door to take her the next time. When I was alone I'd cry over cheap things breaking, African violets that couldn't be brought back to life after being left too long, after being allowed, by my own negligence, to dry out. I felt closer to my mother than ever that first year after.

Mother was the essence of blue.

I don't say anything when he reaches the table.

"It's a client. I told him to call Monday. I told him I wasn't working."

"It's okay. I had a smoke," I say.

He frowns. I quit long ago, actually, before he married me. I don't know why I've started back.

We are here because of our daughter's school—it's a good one in New Orleans, private, but it stops at eighth grade, and she can go to a private high school or to the competitive public one she has qualified for, and Gerald, who lives now in Mobile, came over to discuss this.

He should have remarried, we both know that. Alabama

has plenty of tanned women in sarong skirts who make a career of how they look, who are raised to serve their husband's interests, to drive Jaguars and have gorgeous children who always sleep in nightgowns. New Orleans has even more. He could look. But when he comes to pick up Juliana I think he lingers unnecessarily at the door. He asked for a cup of coffee in my kitchen, recently. The drive back, he said, he didn't want to fall asleep. He sat down to drink it. He didn't have to do that. And we could have gone to any dive or café to discuss Juliana's schooling, but we are in this place which is so famous, on the top of a hotel, where we have so many waiters you have to shoo them away. He chose it. There could be several reasons. I should be trying to figure this out. It is another riddle.

He says, "You started up again?" in a tone I almost recognize as my father's—that Middle South Protestant resignation, so unlike the excitement I sometimes find in men in this town, who seem to have a zest for things that will hurt them, who like to woo their own ruination and wish that you would come along. And if you won't willingly, they'll drag you.

We discuss the schools—Newwell and McCollam, Trinity, the Catholic academies, the public school. He's more interested in the public one than I expected, not because he's cheap, but because it is "more like the real world," he's saying now, and he knows, he lives in the real world, more than when we were married. That's a consequence. So do I. So do I. Being divorced is more real than being married, these days.

I thought I had a reason to be optimistic. My mother always came back, sometimes after a day or two or three, but she came, to our kitchen, to Clara or Sophie or May, whoever was our maid that year—she fired many, and many left, because she was hard to work for, I guess that's clear. She looked beautiful to me at a distance, coming up the walk, her roundness swathed in some dark draped color, or black. She'd wear a jacket or she'd wear a hat. But something would be wrong close up.

My mother's looks comprised the state of the world to me then.

Lipstick smeared, a dirty blouse, a run in her taupe hose, up high on the calf by the seam. When I'd see the flaw, when she'd come home, just like I knew she would but didn't say—it might break the spell—my heart would sink, the universe would collapse. She'd stay up late drinking tea that wasn't really tea. She'd sit in a chair, her legs so far apart, I could see her garters. She didn't care. She smoked like a chimney.

The nothing that she claimed, at first, to be wrong, grew

in the room. It grew the way shadows did in the afternoon, when the sun had abandoned the big windows, and slipped down below the rail on the porch.

"Your father," she'd say very late when we were alone, long after she'd given the maid extra money, handing no one an explanation. "Wants to own me where I live. He does. I'm not letting him. And where is he—where is he?"

Off being important, of course.

When we were in our twenties in Metairie, a suburb, Gerald would be dressing to go into New Orleans and leave me alone with Juliana and the other wives in that little complex with the flimsy wrought iron balconies. I'd tell him, "Being selfish is breathing to you," and he'd wave his long arms and put one hand behind his head and say, "How? Why do you think I work?"

"Are you BLIND?" I would ask Gerald, standing there in the doorway, the hanging ferns falling in my eyes, Juliana in my arms in the clothes she had slept in.

"Show me what I don't see," he'd say, "for crying out loud."

In one way, I didn't think a man, any man, could stand the truth.

In another, I didn't think I could risk telling it.

"Elizabeth?" Gerald is speaking to me. "Did you want

anything else? Earth to Elizabeth," he says, something from a sitcom, I'm sure, he watches them a lot, Juliana told me. When she visits him in Mobile, he doesn't cook. He takes her out to a little beignet and cafe au lait place they have in Mobile, so she will feel "at home"—she's a sophisticated young lady, now, she's a New Orleanian. He lets her drink *coffee*. He adores her.

"I'll have dark roast," I say. Back to the subject. "Her friends will probably all go to McCollam, except the really smart ones."

"My point," he says, "I want her to go to New England for college, I want her to be with the smartest ones. I mean Smith or Mt. Holyoke or even Yale, or Bryn Mawr," he says.

I don't say Bryn Mawr's in Pennsylvania. New England is really a state of mind, not a place, when you are this far south.

I can hear my father when he gets home at night, upstairs, shouting at Mother, "Do you have any idea how this looks? You think you are getting away with this?"

I run down the long hall. I'm holding my ears.

Gerald's standard line was, "Let yourself go."

"Go where?" I finally said back. "Don't tell me where to go." Where, in that apartment with its thin walls and its short hallway, and Juliana, a baby, two or three, ready to wail any minute, or come tell us her nightmares, and me wanting to know what they were, anything to get off the subject. The subject being where should I go according to him. According to him.

"It seems a little stacked," I say to Gerald. "You have made up your mind, haven't you?"

"I didn't think you wanted her to spend her high school years—" he starts in, hesitates.

"What?" I say in an old tone.

"Turning into some little, some purely social being. With the private schools, there's the danger—"

"What danger?"

"That she'll end up like we did, don't you think? Don't they all go to get ensconced in that? Marrying people just like themselves. From the same narrow world, not knowing there is any other? It's as if there's a spell on them, how people surrender to the past here, I am starting to think. It almost always wins."

And he's right.

But I am running down the hall, still, holding my ears.

"Nothing's more important than for her to take herself seriously, I'm quoting," he goes on.

"Who said that?" I ask.

"You. I'm quoting you."

This is where I begin to know I don't know what will happen next. He is being very straight, very sincere. I can tell. Also kind.

There was a harshness back then, when we were breaking up, when she was five, an irony in his voice, when I said I had to take myself seriously, and couldn't be his little wife. And Gerald would say—"What do you mean 'go where?' That's not how I meant it."

"I know Juliana does take herself seriously," I say, putting my cup down in the saucer, causing the slightest splash, but Gerald does not seem to mind my lack of ladylikeness to-night. In fact I get the feeling he likes me just the way I am, looser all together and entirely on my own. That's what he had meant.

"I believe she does too," he says, being dear. "Is there really anything to argue about?" He's smiling. His eyes are big. "Didn't you say she wants to go to the public school but she's not sure?"

Let myself go, I might go crazy. My mother did, quietly, in her room, finally—as long as she stayed in the house, okay. As long as she appeared in public in one piece now and then if my father wanted, then okay.

"Juliana knows what she wants. She takes after her mother," he says.

I'm not like my mother, I am thinking. She was the way all women were supposed to be—weak, hysterical, corrupt, ripe for slaps, escapist, Scarlett, Blanche, all that. I know this is the 1990s. But he's right, nothing ever seems to die out in New Orleans. Everything is chronic. Even the reign of those old gals. I really don't take after my mother. Especially since I'm on my own. I don't.

He grabs the check. The last time I let him buy me food was the day I saw the lawyer. But why not, I think. I don't protest. I feel odd, momentarily beyond it.

I'm also a little queasy, like, seasick.

"She's so amazing," he says, standing, "you've done an incredible job. You have. Listen."

And now, I don't want to argue with him, because we do agree, and it is Juliana. We stroll through that beautiful place, saying goodnight to so many waiters I feel embarrassed. I can tell I'm about to say something, either stupid or brilliant, I'm still not sure which. The urge is irresistible.

We glide down in the slow glass atrium elevator, and the lights lining the riverbank make a snaky cascade outside the window. "What has got you tonight, Elizabeth? What are you thinking about?"

I wish I could concentrate entirely on this extraordinary view, this height, this moment. We had our honeymoon near here at a little hotel, the Cornstalk. Once I remember, when he was with me, I leapt right out of myself, reaching blind, for every dimension of the room at once. I even found them. But afterwards, something had been stolen from me. I felt completely lost. "What is it, Elizabeth?" he asked me, just exactly what he's saying this minute. But he's not upset, right now. You can tell he just wants to know.

When I said and did certain things, when I told him to go, he acted like a man, out of pride. But his pride now breathes. I could walk right through it. And he'd still be there on the other side. I wish I didn't know this.

He was there when I had Juliana. He was there in the hospital's silly yellow paper gown, saying he wanted to be, watching me sweat her out, it felt like, terrible wave by terrible wave. And so I say, off the top of my head, I can't help it, as the elevator lands and opens into a lush green lobby, "You remember when she was born? You remember that day?"

"I do, I never saw you so happy," he says, just as the doors open, as we begin to stroll by the closing shops, the newsstands, the places that sell pralines and Tabasco. "I felt as if I had never made you happy any other time, it was the only day, her little face in that white blanket—" His voice cracks a little when he says this.

We push the brass and glass doors out.

Now we are walking on Royal, into the Quarter, where the past has a life of its own, so says the new slogan. And in the distance, a street saxophonist, but we can't see him. We are completely, impossibly alone.

I hear myself saying, "I wouldn't let you make me happy in those days."

"I know," he says, his face so sweet, so ready, I can hardly bear it. He waits a beat. He doesn't walk. He stands there, asking for my attention. "What's wrong with now?"

"I can't be sure," I have to say.

"Still?" he asks me.

That's when I get the answer. The river has to be its waters, where they go. It isn't its banks even here, where they make so much ado about shoring them up. The river floods. The levees crumble. The gates break down. New Orleans turns into Venice. There are boats in the streets, gondolas with paddle wheels, lovers serenaded by blues musicians, zydeco stars. Odds are sometime in my life this will happen. Some people might find it marvelous, I see that. And others would be overwhelmed, utterly overwhelmed.

Still.

# I AM ELEVEN

Once, when I am eleven, my mother drives up to our house, and parks, and then she doesn't get out of the car. She sits, just sits in her very old maroon and white Chrysler New Yorker with the bulging rear like the rounded haunches on a cherry roan. She broods: she will not come inside.

When I go out to ask her what's wrong, she says if she gets out of the car the reality will all "sink in." When she has to answer the phone, when people speak to her, when Mrs. Fakhouri calls about putting something in the paper—the facts will become more solid than they already are. My mother tells me, "I just cannot bear anything being any clearer."

She doesn't even have to go to the powder room as she calls it. She's staying out there, no matter what, somehow, I can tell. So I go back inside.

A little later, I know without looking my mother has

started smoking because I hear her turn on the car so the lighter will heat up. This takes a long time. When I go out to see her the second time, I lie when she asks me and say there are no matches in the house. "You'll have to come in and turn on the eye of the stove for a light," I say. I hate that she smokes. After that, every time I hear the engine kick in, though, I half-expect her to zoom off. Maybe I want her to. If my mother drives away then her view of the tragic quality of recent events will dissolve, I think, like the smoke does above the Chrysler. This mood of hers will stir itself up in the thin air, and lift, then the good can show. I can rejoice. There is good in everything, I know that, even in trag-edy—my Episcopal Sunday school teacher says so. When something is lost, something else is always gained, that is nature, the law of all life. I am sure of this. I am proud to be young. The news my mother has that day is not tragic.

According to my mother, Coach Whitehall, Mr. Neil Fak-houri, and my father, my brother Randall is going to marry because Linda Fakhouri is expecting to have his baby. Based on the Walt Disney movie about what you do with Kotex, not upon anything my mother has actually told me—this is a small town in South Louisiana in 1968, and mothers do not tell their daughters anything, so that the life of adults is to us a liquid mystery, always dark and interesting and possibly inconceivably dangerous—I think of it in a slightly different way: my brother's baby is growing like a little seedling unfurling from an acorn inside Linda's stomach. I know more or less how it got there, the way you know the secrets people are keeping from you, the way they come to you in your dreams, the way you can know them better than the things they say, how their silence actually outlines perfectly the shape of what they will not tell you.

I have a friend who is thirteen. She says that intercourse is the right word to use. But to me that does not sound like love, it sounds like something public and somewhat unappetizing although perhaps delicious. I am not sure. It sounds as if it is done standing up. Which sometimes it is, my girlfriend has told me.

I guess I understand, even that afternoon, more or less, how it is done in bed, except the mechanics of the man being hard are something I don't quite get. (For how long is he hard? Does he fill and then empty? If he empties, where does all of it go?) But I cannot even imagine Randall in bed with Linda, an alternate cheerleader, even though that must have been the situation, they must have gotten into a bed together. Once. It must have been just once. Perhaps this took place in Lafayette where things are looser. Lafayette is full of dancehalls and Cajuns and wild people. Lafayette one night after an exhibition football game in May, perhaps. If it was not in a bed, then it must have been in a car, then that would have been intercourse, in the most certainly awful way, that would have been something public and obscene but I know in my heart it is nothing like that.

It upsets me to even think these things while I look out the bay window of my father's study at the street where my mother is. I am positive my brother and Linda have come together as virgins.

After a while, this becomes a serious problem to me—getting my mother out of the old Chrysler with pigskin laced to the steering wheel where she has been staring ahead and smoking since around one o'clock, upon her return from the meeting with the coach and my father and Randall and Linda's father and Linda. The coach was there, my mother explains to me my third time out to visit her, because, well, Coach Whitehall knows these two are "fine young people," and he wanted to say a few words. He felt responsible, and he thought he could act, my mother says, in a ridiculing way, as a "buffer." The coach discovered the situation when he had a "heart-to-heart" with Randall about his not putting his all into football practice. For forty minutes I stand beside her in the shade of the oak tree, clasping her cool small hand through the open window, listening to every detail of the meeting, descriptions of the Fakhouris, Coach Whitehall, Randall's sad expression, Linda, beaming.

My mother goes on and on, in a way I don't understand completely, scattering the story through torrents of talk—Randall when he was a baby, Randall when she had his photo taken in that little cowboy suit, that poor girl—Linda, that woman, not even American, Catholic and Syrian, for God's sakes, no, Lebanese. "Love they say, love they call it," she says and she will not get out of the car, no matter what I suggest. I can't listen any longer, because it makes me want to cry, and I'm not even sure why, my mother's being so sad, and so full of all those moments of the past, and clear about them. But I will not believe it isn't love.

All this time, I, Ariel McKinley, am thrilled, if the truth be known. If this is happening, if my brother is going to be a father, there must be some reason for it in the overall plan, which I know is there—girls know this when they are eleven, that the world is beneficent. I am so absolutely sure.

I go back outside for the fourth time after the afternoon movie. I always get hungry around this time. I beg my mother to come in to eat. I tell her we can sit down with the two ham sandwiches I can make, or whatever it is our housekeeper Josephine has left in the oven my mother will have to tell me how to cook, but my mother says no, she won't come in and see what is in the oven, because she just cannot believe this kind of thing can be happening to her. If she goes in the house, she says she knows the phone will ring, people will ask questions—has she lost Randall really, to that little girl, that dark child?

Yes she has. She will have to say it. That's what she says to me.

She says coming inside would be like walking in on your life and finding it in total, irretrievable ruin.

When my mother finishes her last Parliament, it is seven o'clock. My father has pulled up in his metallic brown-finned Plymouth. It is after Huntley-Brinkley, late dusk. I have answered the telephone twice, both times a woman with an accent on the other end, and I have lied, saying I don't know where my mother has gone. It is Mrs. Fakhouri obviously, but she doesn't introduce herself. I have eaten two bowls of Cocoa Krispies.

I am relieved to see my father because I love him with everything I have. I watch him walk directly from his car to the Chrysler to plead with my mother. He is a tall, gentle man, I think. After he's been with her a while, he comes in the house and has a ham sandwich I've made for him. I ask him should I take my mother out a tray of food. He says, "No, absolutely not."

I go to bed at nine-thirty, usually, but I cannot sleep at all. At ten-thirty I can still hear my father out there yelling (this is rare, this is very rare) and weeping (even rarer, only at my grandfather's funeral has my father wept in my lifetime), and even later I look outside to see him kissing my mother's hands, and getting inside the car and then getting out. Finally after I've gone to sleep, I wake and he's inside the house with her, at something after midnight.

My mother is wailing and sobbing downstairs in the den.

The whole neighborhood has probably heard my parents carrying on, but not the exact content, not the words. It is a long time before I know all of what my father has said, what my mother has said. What has really happened between them. It's months before I know anything, really. It's the night Linda's going to deliver, in fact.

The next day mostly all I can think is that there is going to be a baby in the house, a baby. I have never felt luckier. It does occur to me how my brother will not be my brother anymore. I imagine he'll be holding a diaper, he'll have pins in his mouth, he won't be around to take the Cocoa Krispies down for me from the highest shelf. He is six feet two, and he can do things like that when he is in a good mood. But when I weigh these things against a baby and a sister-in-law, they are not much, I decide.

* * *

The marriage of my brother two weeks later is as awful as intercourse: open, public, embarrassed, without love. It is even perhaps filthy: my father thinks so, he makes awful attempts at jokes. Mr. Fakhouri tries to smile. He fascinates me—his teeth so perfectly white and numerous, his eyes round and dark. My mother tells my father at that lunch, actually, in public, to "shut up" and his face collapses for a second. I feel this deeply, like something closing in around my lungs.

There are many rooms in our house, more than my mother ever even bothered to decorate. She left some undone, the doors usually shut, and the shades pulled down, and inside there are squares of yellow-pink light, one for every window, its match, thrown down on the floor, and stray pieces of furniture, old dressers, unhung prints and mirrors with pretty frames.

Our house is the kind of place you can hide very well in, if you want to, and you are a child. But once Linda moves in, I run into her everywhere. Linda seems lost, not hidden.

The first time we are alone, Linda tells me she and Randall were married by a Unitarian minister (they are the kind who will do anything ), months before, in Biloxi, in a beach cottage. Way last spring. I am so relieved. They planned to keep this secret until Randall got into college. Then she got pregnant totally by mistake. They married first for love. This is so good to believe.

The two rooms for the couple are Randall's old bedroom, with pennants from the Dallas Cowboys, and from LSU and Tulane (like all big, smart boys, Randall is supposed to grow up to play football in college and then become a lawyer) and the long sleeping porch we weren't using, so big and hot it takes two window units. Linda decides to make this porch the sitting room and future nursery. Randall says, "fine," but Linda and I do all the work, while her other half sits downstairs with our father that first weekend Linda is in the house, watching golf reruns. Coach Whitehall has come to Monday's wedding—it was just for show, for the parents, for them, Linda's told me—but my brother has still done terribly Friday night against the team from Eunice, so badly that he sat out the last quarter. If this keeps up, they will not go to the state championships and therefore Randall is very depressed. He doesn't want to fix up any sitting room. He eats chips with our daddy. They watch Sam Snead.

The transformation of the sleeping porch involves getting a couch out at Lemoine's Used Furniture and begging Randall to help us haul it up the stairs before my mother comes back from visiting her mother in a nursing home over in La

Grange. Finally Randall does what we ask late that Saturday afternoon, but once he has it on the second floor, he leaves us to drag it across the hall while he goes downstairs again. He does all this without putting down the apple in his hand—some things about my brother drive me perfectly nuts. Sometimes I hate his ease in the world, his notion that everything is his unless you tell him differently. Sometimes I hate how much he eats. But he can eat all he wants, and so what, he is a boy. How boys always take what they need is what we are supposed to love about them somehow. I try to see it.

Except for the fact that he makes Linda "do it three times a night"—Linda tells me, my brother doesn't appear to care if she is alive or not, but that's only on the surface, I think. He's embarrassed by his desperate love: this is a secret I know.

There are many long afternoons that hot fall, in the pink sleeping porch where nobody sleeps, and we set up an old table in front of the black plastic covered "modern style" used couch. Linda plays Ike and Tina Turner over and over, and Randall's and her song, "The Letter" by the Box Tops. She plays records by the Tams and the Platters and Otis Redding and she plays "Louie Louie." She wears shorts and her slick black hair is up in brush rollers—it is vehemently straight, and coarse and thick, and all brush rollers will do for it is give it something called "body," which lasts about one hour and a half, and she does her nails and wears fuzzy slippers all day—she's quit high school, of course—and at night when Randall is up there and she says things like "God, God, God, and Lord, Lord, Lord," and then she gives one of her wails of pleasure or pain, I am never sure which, even though Linda has told me in a general way what all the steps are to the climax.

The climax is what adults know children do not know, I decide. It is the dividing line.

In those early dusky evenings, when Vietnam comes on the TV, Randall and Linda start in upstairs after Randall comes home from football practice, and I am sure my parents know they do it constantly. It is obvious. Sometimes you can hear the headboard clattering against the wall, big as that house is.

At night, in the dark, it is even more common, and louder, somehow, no other daily sounds to get in the way. I worry about my mother in her room directly across the hall. She is far away all this time, my mother is, even though she's in the house. It is very hard to get her attention. She drives places without telling us where.

I even watch my brother and Linda one night in October and it is either obscene or luscious. I see them by mistake but afterwards I think about it a lot. I think of my brother's mouth, especially, wide open when he is finally where he wants to be. He's so loud, like a warrior, and anguished-sounding, and then there's Linda, in her interesting pain, perhaps. Actually, sometimes I think "pain" and sometimes I think not.

My brother's mouth is wide open as he stands there in his underwear. He seems so interested in this, in swaying back and forth with her in front of his dresser our mother bought him when he was thirteen. Nothing in the world has ever been so interesting to my brother as this. She backs onto the bed.

I am looking through the crack in the pink bathroom door. I can only see certain things, such as my brother's fanny, and Linda's tiny green see-through babydoll pajamas. Then he rolls on top of her, and buries himself in Linda's scanty clothes, and I can see Linda's round little acorn belly in that light, as they lie crosswise, over the bed, her knees up now, her groaning, but her eyes have a faraway look (it isn't even really night, it is still light enough to see that Linda's eyes are brown—they do this when it isn't night). Randall's mouth is open so wide, that I am, there for a minute, frightened of him and not interested in this sort of business, this kissing and burying. I think it is going to make me throw up to watch.

I know they must bother my mother. It sounds so much like agony—Linda bites her lip and bites my brother's back, and almost weeps with something like frustration, anger, energy—but when I talk to Linda she says that is ecstasy, ecstasy is a fact of the climax, which is what you do the whole thing for. The object of every act, what everything grown-ups do turns out to be for, is the climax. This I learn, a previously invisible law.

I never really like football. I don't value cheerleading, either, never became one. I go to see Randall play that fall, basically, to be with my father, no other reason. Linda doesn't go like she used to. She can't cheer, and that hurts.

My mother hasn't gone for years. When Randall was on the J. V. team, his coach once had to ask our mother to get off the field when a one hundred-and-sixty-pound ninth grader from the Opelousas High team dug into Randall's calf muscle with a cleat, and Randall passed out from it. My mother, whose name is Kitty, started to scream at the coach, asking him what he thought he was doing, overseeing the maiming and slaughter of innocents.

So when I don't go, then my father is up there in the stands alone. He favors Wally Cox, people say, about my father. I know he is much better looking. I love the narrow, acute type of man my father is. He likes to have me with him. When I see him my heart sings too. I am his buddy.

At the games, there is a whole group of older girls, eighth graders, who start saying awful things about Linda Fahkouri. They love my brother to death, besides. These are the girls who smoke, write on bathroom mirrors with lipstick, and stand talking under the stands, their little breasts brushing up against their boyfriends' chests as they lean on posts, and giggle. These girls have everything, do everything the way they are supposed to, go far enough, not too far. They are popular, pretty.

All I am in their eyes is Randall McKinley's sister.

In December Linda shows me the dress she wore to their secret wedding the spring before down in Biloxi. It's an A-line of white eyelet over yellow kettle cloth. She tells me how happy they were then, how their two nights, no, four nights, alone in the beach house were heaven on earth. That first, true marriage has taken place somewhere that is not Lamarck. It happened in Mississippi where the trees are darker and the passions are stronger, not in Lamarck in the Episcopal minister's study, in a cold public longsleeves situation, where nobody smiled or seemed to express joy, including my own brother, who never seemed so depressed as he did at that wedding, in his whole life except for twice: when he was six and a girl beat him wrestling after he made her eat a dog biscuit, and once when he fumbled a ball in a J. V. football game against Clinton, costing his team three points. But since Linda and Randall were married in heaven before they were married on earth, I know the love my brother has for Linda deep down is exactly the love I have hoped for. It has never been *intercourse* but love, pure love, sweet as Romeo and Juliet, minimum, Linda says. I ardently believe, those shorter afternoons around Christmas while we listen to the Box Tops and Linda, seven months along, pops Dentyne gum so she'll have sweet breath when Randall comes home.

I tell the eighth grade girls who'll listen all about the secret wedding. I tell them in the bathroom during the Winter Dance in the gym. They lean against the sinks, with their Tareyton smokes, inhaling French. One of them, I can see her now, can raise one eyebrow very high and not the other. She starts to say something, but I say, "I know it's true, I know it's true."

"Okay," she says. She shuts up.

Linda is big by New Year's, and he doesn't want to do it anymore. So Randall is unhappy, and I am relieved. The bigger she gets, the more Linda speaks of it: love love love, undying, love without end. The secret wedding gets better and better, Linda tells me more about it, it is more lavish. I find out they spent more days in the beach house.

Then it is the end of February, just like that, as if no time has passed at all and we are in the parish hospital. I sit with my father while Linda is in the ward. My mother is in Birmingham. Daddy starts to tell me things he probably shouldn't tell, about how Randall has had a horrible year, and perhaps, now, it can be over, the baby will have a name. He says nothing kind about Linda. He takes this for granted, and I am supposed to know that the world works this way, and not that, that my brother can be in La Grange where they don't card you, drinking with his friends if he wants to be. And Linda is the one that is all bad. He can have girlfriends, too, my father doesn't fault Randall, it is a monstrous thing, being a father at eighteen, Daddy says. He keeps saying he will call Randall soon, and get him down to the hospital, but he never does. Randall has lost his youth, he says. It is so rotten, he says. Randall needs to sow his wild oats, he says.

My father tells me these things perhaps knowing, sensing that in my heart I have taken Linda's side. Maybe he is trying to win me back, especially that night, with Linda in labor, in so much pain we brought her.

I tell him about how they really married last spring and for love. It is a secret, but I've already told at school, so I tell it. I feel I have to. My father doesn't know about true love, and I do.

When I'm done he looks at me like I'm grown, and it's a joke, and he says, "You believe that?" and I'm supposed to get it all. "Oh, Arelee," he chortles, using my nickname. From when I was so little. The one he gave me. "Honey—"

Then, deliberately, it isn't nice, he starts in about that first day, last August, when we could not get my mother out of the Chrysler. He says he finally had to grab her wrists, and say, "Kitty, I am your husband. Listen to me. You have to come in. I am ordering you!" and my mother says to him— this is the part my father finds amusing, " 'The way you are, that's what is wrong, Randall is a man now. I never wanted this to happen, Randall to turn into a man. I am not prepared for Randall to turn into a man.' "

My father almost starts to laugh. "What did she think? What did she expect?" he asks me. "What am I?" he asks me.

And just then for a minute everything depends upon me.

You see, somehow, when I get the joke, when I answer, it will be funnier. We can laugh together.

"Your mother was actually trying to kick me, I didn't let her," he goes on with this odd, mean smile. "She'd have liked to kill me. She would have."

My father is depending upon me at least to begin a grin. "I dragged her. I had to. Dragged her out of that car. Had to."

By now, we have already been waiting a long, long time, and soon Linda Fakhouri McKinley, all by herself, will bear the huge perfect baby Randall McKinley the Third. But I'm not supposed to think about Linda. I'm supposed to think about my daddy and what he wants, his thin, lined features practically praying to me to smile. "Pulled her by the wrists, she wouldn't pick up her feet. Your mamma—"

The climax must have taught my father what that was, what was so funny about him dragging my mother into the house. It must have shown him the fact that things that sound hateful are really hilarious, that pain is secretly plea-sure—this is what goes through my mind. And since I, Ariel McKinley, haven't had one, I have no idea in this world how I am supposed to smile. When I grow up I'll know how what he's told me is funny, I figure. The knowledge will come to me when I am a woman like Linda, when pain is all blended in with love. But I can't do what he wants, not this time, not at all. I have to get up and walk away from him toward Linda's ward. One time I turn around to look, and he's still waiting for me to smile. I stare.

As I tell this now it's as if I'm still looking right back at my father, no words, no amusement, ever arriving on my lips. My face is blank as the mirrors were in all those roomy rooms my mother couldn't finish.

I wonder if he believed I could still love him the same.

# CROCHETING

I am crocheting a blue wool hat for my mother because of what is happening to her. Her head is a gray balloon: her eyes swim at the top of her face like two small fish. Her skin is hard from the tugging and swelling caused by the drugs she takes which are meant to reduce the mass of knotted veins around her tumors.

Crocheting is a system of knots made with one string and one needle, over and over, invented by fishing net knotters' wives who wanted to make nets for their tables and one-needle lace for the ends of their collars and curtains, for the hems of their children's clothes. On the French Atlantic Coast the fishermen drag scallops and fishes and mussels up in white nets. On the high hill overlooking the sea, a child huddles under a shawl next to his mother who is looking westward at the Atlantic and hoping that the wind will go back up into the sky.

This hat is sky blue, and so is the scarf already finished. The scarf is rounded like a stole instead of flat as something woven because I failed to count the stitches. One extra or two too few and a scarf meant to be straight becomes round and gathered, somehow irregular. If you split yarn with the needle even once, however, it will be impossible to unravel back to your mistake.

I went to see her Tuesday. The thin doctor at the door waved his hand and said it was fine for us to go to the gift shop downstairs on the G floor of Oncology. Mother wanted to buy a card to thank people for seeing her. She knows it is difficult to come, to look at her.

It is a famous and enormous hospital in New Orleans. Outside, behind the terraced plaza for the Cancer Wing is a heliport. There is a brick wall around it, but I imagine it is a phosphorescent target, a cross in a circle, painted on tar. I was afraid of holding her elbow, of holding her anywhere. My boyfriend Jerome told me he saw on her chart that she would be brittle now, and later, more so.

When we walked into the shop, several people stared at her pinkish cowl-necked robe, at her bare, bald, marked head.

She is decorated with purple marks like the painted de-signs on the bodies of the Natchez and the Moundbuilders as they have been rendered in watercolors by the French explorers. She noticed this in the mirror and said, "See, I told you I was a pagan." The lines are meant to show the X-ray therapists where, exactly, to irradiate her. There are borders, axes, and faded circles, all over her bald head.

Her skull is very large, hard, difficult to kiss. Her cheeks are taut as leather. But the rest of her body is slack and insubstantial. It is in the process of wizening. She shuffled into the elevator next to me. She leaned toward me to tell me she was happy to see me, which she was.

I am always afraid to see her.

I learned to crochet when I was nine. My French grandmother, her mother, now dead of aneurysms and Pall Malls, taught me as she had learned it from her grandfather, who was a man who could make wine from greens, liquor from berries, mend his own shirts. He came over here from France because people spoke the language. My grandmother taught me to hold the needles the wrong way—parallel for knitting, and upside down for crochet. I have never been able to learn the proper way, and thus to understand the elaborate photographs and diagrams which explain new stitches in the pattern books. I've never learned anything much beyond chain, double and treble. Popcorn and feather stitching, possible with a single hook, have always been impossible for me to understand. See, my grandmother never told me to count. She said to answer all the stitches I had in the following row, and not to make any new ones, unless you are adding them to make a hat, which is a spiral, unless you know what you are doing. "You go by the rhythm," she told me. "You feel awry if you skip a stitch."

Sometimes I feel this, sometimes I don't.

In the needlework shops uptown on Magazine, I am a left-handed child. "Who taught you to hold a needle like that? Where do you hold the yarn for tension?" I use my thumb. "Valerie, look. Come look at this!" the clerk shouts to the needlework teacher in the back room. I always leave.

I am crocheting a blue wool hat for my mother because she is dying of cancer in the bone and the spine and skull. The hat should be soft on her scalp which itches because her hair is at best a fine stubble, and all new every few weeks. It grows in between the radiation treatments. The doctor said three days ago that she was lucky. She wouldn't have to drink the chemotherapy doses any longer. They could inject them directly into the spine now. They will use a spongy implant called a reservoir, which they sewed into the top of her brain last week. That dispelled all the marijuana and leukemia stories I might have told her before I gave her a joint. She doesn't need any. She has an appetite, and no nausea, but she also has this steely pain I have no idea about. She seems to have less and less daylight in her. I keep thinking of trying to do something to pry all this misery away from her, but I am perfectly aware that if I touch her she will break.

She has one single long window that reminds me of the narrow, very modern doctor who left healthy people to do further training here at Tulane as an oncologist. All his patients behind the open doors on her corridor have grayish skin with a blue glaze, and the same oceanic eyes. They are suspended, half-hoping to be let go, I think. Waiting for him to be done with them. The window looks out on the concrete shelves that will one day be another wing of the hospital, which is encroaching upon the sadder end of Canal Street, about ten blocks from the Quarter. Next to it, there is a bulletin board, filled with notes from all of us: thank-you notes, get-well notes, printed pictures of bouquets, pictures of candles and Mary. One of my grandmother's sisters used to buy our family novenas for Christmas. Mother would take a crinkly ribbon in the old days, punch a hole above the Mary on the novena card, string it through and hang it on the tree. Later she'd tell me it made her nervous to know a group of nuns in Grand Cotou were rising nine mornings in a row to pray for our names. But lately, she does not seem to mind as much. She even told me there was a priest who talked to her one night in the hospital and it was okay.

I would buy her a novena if I knew who was selling them.

My grandmother was interested in heaven. On the night she died, my mother sat with her. Grandmother announced she was already in heaven—it looked like the green gardens of Jackson Square in front of St. Louis Cathedral—she said this as she passed in and out of consciousness, and in and out of breath. She had double pneumonia on top of the aneurysms already in her chest. "Heaven is beautiful," she reported to Gloria, my mother, whose head is now a silverish balloon, whose eyes float like two sea twins, whose body is shrinking under her odd, out-of-style pink robe. Grandmother even greeted her long-dead brother Phillippe, someone she never really liked in life. He was walking over toward her across that well-planted park. "I like heaven, it's beautiful," she told my mother, who believes ultimately that when she leaves she leaves sans everything, so she was standing next to me in the gift shop staring at the gold chains and the bad prints of the hospital and the tacky New Orleans souvenirs, as if she meant to memorize every object, as if she wanted to know how every trinket came into being, to understand how every shell on a chain in the glass case below us came up out of the gulf in a net and landed here.

Grandmother's dying was a supernatural event. I remember being in her house shortly afterwards and trying to find her. I needed her then, I was sixteen, and she was my connection to so many things. This was on Freret, where she lived in a duplex, not that far from our house. I finally decided she had amplified, and dispersed. She had atomized, turned into everything else even the air and the water in the kettle. My sister brought a twelve-day-old infant to the funeral. Her own. The old ladies at the parlor said, something like that always happens, that a baby is born in a family when someone dies. To me Grandmother was not really in the box, but released—or maybe I imagined this. The funeral over her body was slightly irrelevant, for someone else. My sister and I smiled at one another, and laughed, and played hearts the day after, made a fantastic gumbo. We tickled the baby who cried and coughed at night like a monkey. My sister, who refused to nurse, complained that her breasts were killing her. "You have no idea," she told me about childbirth. "You have no idea how it really is. You enter another dimension. Or it enters you. You can't even tell. What you think you are just vanishes. What you ever thought you were, it doesn't exist." She was proud and furious over this, I could see, both at once. I probably will be too.

Right after the burial, there were distant members of the family and neighbors in a line to tell me that they all "loved me very much," and I was drunk with taking their hands and putting myself in their arms. And then I was holding my mother awkwardly around the neck. My watch got caught in the crocheted shawl she wore over her head because she was once a Catholic. I think she pried me away.

Mother doesn't watch television in the room when she is alone. Neither does she crochet, which is something that skips a generation. When every stitch is filled in, there is no pattern at all, only a monotony: the incestuous danger of too many repetitions. My mother has always seemed to think this was a special danger, too many repetitions. When we moved back to New Orleans, when I was twelve, after trying St. Paul and California, she felt defeated. My father stayed in L. A. So we'd lost our male, we'd lost our possibility of Lighting Out for the Territory. She still calls our return to the city of her birth "the Descent."

But that was how *she* saw it.

Novenas are interesting to me, quaint. Lourdes water is appealing, like my grandmother's upside-down method of working. So are Medjugorje, all sightings of the virgin, most Catholic things about New Orleans, the entire idea of God having to have a mother.

But when my mother dies, I don't know if it will be a supernatural event. She doesn't think it will. And I am inclined to think the way she does, now, somehow, when I am with her. She is in that room, and in that body, which they are poisoning daily into something else, and I am afraid that she will die inside it as she is. There will be nothing more. Her head will continue to swell and her spine may break, and her bones will become more brittle, and then, after morphine elixirs and what they call extraordinary measures at this famous hospital, they will finally allow her to go. I have this feeling. That it is a matter of permission.

Right now I am crocheting a hat for her head in case she makes it until the winter. It isn't such a winter here in New Orleans, but there are wet days, there are chills, there are spotty, swirly rains. Recently they told her they will allow her to go home until she has healed enough to stand more treatments. This winter she should be warm. The stitch is three trebles in a row, skip a beat, three more, which is called the scallop stitch. Little hands or fans move in a spiral more or less outward from the top of her head where her soul, according to legend, will flutter out for heaven, a place she never particularly liked. They have allowed her to go home and this winter she should be warm. The stitch is three trebles in a row, skip a beat, three more, all into the same spot, skip a beat, chain, three more, which is called the scallop stitch. Little hands or fans move in a spiral outward from the top of her head where her soul, according to legend, according to belief, will flutter out for heaven, a place she was never particularly interested in. Little hands or fans move in a spiral outward from the top of her head, where her soul, according to legend, will flutter out for heaven, a place she never believed in, even after her mother told her it looked just like the grounds at Jackson Square on a sunny day.

Jerome didn't say he read this, but I think that before she dies her skull will soften like a baby's and maybe she will need that crocheted cap to hold in her ideas, to remind her that her name is Gloria, and that I am her daughter, really. It is hard to contemplate, if you look at it straight on, I think. I could see forgetting these connections, as they can be a burden.

I am afraid to touch her head when I go see her. It is swollen, it is a silver balloon. Her eyes float above the center like two sea twins. Above them are the gentian violet targets.

Grandmother left my mother novenas in perpetuity, like scratched records repeating over and over into infinity *Mother of Grace*. On Tuesday, after a while, my mother shuffled over to the card counter in the hospital gift shop to read everything on display: "To Dad on your 25th Anniversary"; "To a Beloved Mother-in-Law, Get Well"; "Grandmother, Our Sympathy"; "Congratulations on your Bundle of Joy." Mother counted the syllables or the verses as she read them to me, unconsciously, with her mouth, knowing when they felt wrong. That sort of rightness is in her like the regularity of the stitches made of a single waltzed string. But if I mentioned it, that that rhythm is something Grandma had, she'd look at me a certain way. One two three. Every row must be the same number of stitches if the fabric is to stay flat. I don't often get it right. I see my mother got it, but she didn't pass it on to me.

In a spiral hat, the added stitches do not matter as much. In fact, you have to add them, more and more, in order to allow the hat to grow larger. If you don't the hat becomes a tightened mass impossible to unravel as her tumors. You have to cut the yarn and start over again if you don't continually expand from the star-like caesura at the top of the head where the soul is supposed to come and go. Spirals are easier for me.

Now the hat is finished. I'm trying to tie it off. It is lopsided. She will probably say oh how nice, when I give it to her tomorrow. She will tug it over her scalp and her watery eyes will narrow. I will hand her a mirror. She will tell me, it's a little lopsided, because that's the kind of person she's always been, the kind who tells you when things are awry. The kind who always notices. Tugging the edge over her left ear, she will probably undo the finishing knot. While I try to think about the amazing truth, that she is my mother, really, that she bore me into the confusing world, that I probably came from the same place she is going to, that she is ahead of me as we pass through these thresholds, maybe she will ravel the spiral backward to the top of her head. She will smile. On the hospital bed between us will be a wad of crinkled sky blue yarn, pure chaos. Maybe I'll promise her I can crochet it again. When she leans over to hug me, I will pause under her thin arms, trying to imagine this—I mean everything, the source, the ending. Trying to really see what this possibly means, that we have travelled to this place and that we are going to leave it, Grandmother coming before us all, all the millions of perfect repetitions, and the thousands of beats that were missed, those too. We'll probably hang on too long. I will have to pry her away. Or she will pry me. This will be awkward, that's how we have always been. She was awkward with her mother, too.

Every day after I see her I take a walk. I go all the way from the hospital's end of Canal through downtown and over to the Quarter, down to the front of the cathedral. I stand there in Jackson Square by the impatiens and the coleus, so neat, perfect little rows of enthusiastic flowers, such a vision of sense. By that time I am usually loving and hating God in absolutely equal amounts. I remind myself He has a mother, too. I try to forgive Him. I try.

# OSLO

One Saturday in December, my husband told me that he wanted to find a place to live that meant something to him. I told him I knew Baton Rouge was still strange to us, but that was not official, it was patter. I wanted to ask him how he broke up with his first wife, for reference. But every time he answers that question the response is different. So we talked about other people: why did the visiting Norwegian artist we liked so much leave town before her stay was properly over? Why did she abandon all her paintings? The recent ugly abstracts and the early works with sheep, some haystacks, tundras in the sun, even fjords but not hokey, were stored hastily in our friends the Richardses' garage.

She had hung out with the Richardses and us, and had planned to leave almost a month later, and take her stuff, of course. Roll up the canvases, weigh everything, ship it. Instead, she just took off for the airport Friday morning in a cardigan, her hair curled under at the chin—so pretty, everybody thought—heading for Oslo.

The next day, Nadine Richards came over on a bicycle, in brilliant sweatpants, and sat on a tiled step in our new house, trembling. She called her husband, Jordan, a cad and a creep. He was too silent. He hoarded himself. She didn't know him anymore. He didn't think he wanted to ever have kids. She hated him. And he was in love, she had figured out, with the lady painter who left.

Jordan is a good guy—to this everyone agreed. Even my husband agreed, and he is harsh on people and places. He hates Baton Rouge, for instance. We've lived here a year and a half, and before this San Antonio. We could live somewhere else. Mark is a computer writer. He gives good manual, as he says. He admitted he hated our life before I asked him how he left his first wife. Was his exit gradual or abrupt? Did he know in February and wait until June to do it? Did he know in May and in a week break it off for good? When did he know why he had done it? A year later? At the time? When he met me? Mark answered that he wanted to live either in San Francisco or in Jerusalem. What an address Jerusalem would be, but maybe you wouldn't understand, he told me.

"Oslo," Nadine said loudly, Sunday, over some jazz we

had put on the stereo. In her aerobic pink pants, she seemed to shimmer around the edges—a first-day-of-the-rest-of-your-life look, something in a movie. "I swear I'm telling him to go this time," she then announced. "I know he was in love with her." She picked at the cranberry bread I'd baked, but she wasn't really eating. "I just took it all in on Friday, when he got back from taking her to the airport. She had insisted she was leaving because she couldn't cope with the looks of the subtropics. This town, this place was frightening to her. The banana trees, the catalpas. The lizards that come into your house. Swamps. Such palaver, really. She had to get back to her native landscape. She was losing her connection to things, felt out of time, couldn't paint. I stayed up nights listening to this crock."

It is awfully hot in south Louisiana sometimes in December, I was thinking, watching Nadine perspire. It climbs into the eighties, then there's a cold snap.

Monday morning, I saw Jordan at a sandwich counter next door to the bookstore he manages, and his eyes were dark, as usual, but with new gray circles. He was wearing a white cotton sweater Nadine had knitted, which swallowed him. He felt furtive about seeing even me. I guess I was too well versed in the reasons Nadine and he should split. And I wanted to go up to him and hold his hand, tell him we were there—Mark and I—if he wanted to talk to someone. He sat four seats away from me at the counter and said the merest hello. While I was eating a wet avocado salad, I realized that Jordan had never started a sentence in my presence with the word "I" and gone on to elaborate how he felt. It wasn't in his makeup. What did he know about himself that he couldn't tell anybody?

On Wednesday, I called Nadine and told her she should leave Jordan. Or at least lock him out. She replied that she was going to—going to do the right thing.

"You don't know the half of it," she went on. "He loves to love women he hardly knows. Once he almost left me for a woman whose book he had read. He fell for her through photos and letters. This lady painter will get him to Oslo. Then, once he's there, he'll start hoarding his heart again. It's the proximity he hates."

"So lock the door," I said.

"He won't deny it—he doesn't care what I know," Nadine said. "Won't say it, either." She sucked on a cigarette. (She is the only person left I know who smokes.) "He's got a house key."

"Face it. It's over. He hurts you. You know that," I said. "You've been going on about this for so long. Remember the chalet in Alabama?"

The four of us took a vacation there. It was supposed to be brisk in the southern Appalachians in June. She told me once at breakfast there that he grabbed her at night like a cool pillow—then, in the morning, nothing.

"I know," she said now. "I know it. I've been talking about it for months. Maybe even a year. However long we've been friends. I've got no idea why he likes me, even. I'm not his type."

Then I told Nadine she was being stupid. She is beautiful. Her features are unusual and piquant; her hair is full and well cut. And besides, she is good-natured. She trusts people.

On Thursday, my husband said that Jordan, who is his only friend in town, was just bored. I said Nadine said he was a cad, and then I thought how old-fashioned, Edwardian even, to know a cad. Handsome, black-eyed, ruthless a little, interested in distance in his women, not pleasure. I would love Jordan if he liked me, almost, I thought.

That afternoon, Nadine called me and I told her again to set up barriers. It was the only way. I said I was speaking from experience. Everybody wants what he can't have. I told her to be martial. She couldn't go on as she had been. I mentioned self-respect. She responded that Jordan had admitted he was planning to go to Oslo but that the woman had got skittish about the plan at the end and run away.

Then she said, "He doesn't know what he wants. He came home this morning. Had spent the night out. Sat around like an object. Said nothing. Wouldn't even say where he had slept. Do you know? I told him to move out next month. He said he'd look for a place. But we get along, you know. I don't know how to cook."

"Take yourself seriously," I told her.

"I do," she said. "We're serious. We're just not planning to do it tomorrow. We both work. It's a lot of trouble."

Then I realized Nadine wasn't as angry as she pretended to be. She was just too sad. She was by herself, in her open kitchen, and her husband, Jordan, was in some part of the house, probably sitting under a floor lamp looking at some of the other woman's color slides. He is so large and good-looking that I had a hard time imagining he was also sad. Nadine went on explaining. It didn't matter that he had slept with the painter, it was that he'd kept everything from her. Held back. "Making me the heart police," she said. "And I'm becoming this cold person, somebody I don't even like. This isn't life."

While Nadine was talking to me I was thinking that the rooms in my house were clean and interesting, and I was kind of happy even though we live in Baton Rouge. I had been planning to buy one of the Norwegian woman's paintings, to hang on the brick above our working fireplace. My husband thought the woman talked too much. She reminded him of Liv Ullmann in those Bergman movies. She had odd ideas, and she repeated herself. He asked what did Jordan see in her. Then I thought about having bright blue furniture and living in Jerusalem. We have two cars and inch-wide blinds; these things took on nuance whenever I thought of giving them up. An image of my husband and me sitting down in Israel, near a little balcony, appeared once in a dream of my husband's ex-wife. She was very tall and always had few men to choose from. Even after their divorce, she wanted Mark badly, and snatched him away from me at gallery openings or parties when we were all there together. Yet she had this dream, which she called him about once, early in the morning—woke us up to tell us. It was so vivid, she said, that it seemed painted. She saw my husband and me living in a small white apartment in Jerusalem, with a view of the sea, among cushions the color of lapis lazuli. Mark told her there isn't any sea in Jerusalem. Then he hung up, like that. I knew the history of their unhappiness, the reasons for it, but I could never see him just shut down with her one day and say no more, good-bye. The first several months I knew him, after he had left her, his heart was packed in ice.

I finally told him to thaw or abuse somebody else, and since then he's been at room temperature, with lapses.

Almost at midnight on Thursday, the same day, Nadine called back and said she had been crying. "It's pitch dark in Oslo at this time of year," she said. "Night all the time now. How could a painter go there in December? I bet she's not going to paint anymore. I know it. That's why she left all her work out in our garage. What did Jordan *do* to her? I just realized this. It has taken all week, almost, for it to sink in. I'll feel sorry for her even if he goes to her. Especially if he goes to her. Am I crazy?" she asked, then paused, giving me a chance to catch up and say something, but I didn't; I was thinking about other things. "I feel so far away from this," she continued. "We are in Louisiana and Jordan is in love with this woman who is sitting in a room somewhere six hours into tomorrow, and it is still dark there anyway. And I feel so far away. I could be on the moon tonight. I don't even know if he is sleeping here or going out, is he in the house or not."

"Take a look," I said. "You are okay. Maybe I will come over. Nobody is satisfied. Mark wants to move to Jerusalem. It is a place, he says. You know where you are when you are there. It's a good city to be buried in—lots of company. The world could end there, even. History in the streets. I think he wants to get rid of me. I always thought we had it down."

"I was in Oslo once," Nadine answered. "I was sixteen, on a trip with my parents, who went off on their own, so I walked around on these endless sunny evenings and met polite boys. One of them took me to a museum full of those paintings by Edvard Munch. I knew nothing then, wasn't prepared. On the whole second floor of this museum are pictures the size of double doors filled with people in one kind of obvious pain or another. The figures are so hard and flat and separate. All of them are standing in interiors with harsh colors behind them—this citron yellow representing light from lamps. Hideous. It was as if the backgrounds were mean to them and so they were starting to turn into rocks. Munch and Grieg, the two other artists from Norway. It must feel crucial to be there. Maybe where you were born is essential. Maybe she was telling the truth. In the summer, the sun is relentless; then it just goes out. I don't know. I think I am going crazy. I don't feel like locking Jordan out. I want to send him on. Here there are no seasons at all. It only matters what the day is like. It never goes by the week, even. Tonight it is cold, for once. Jordan's on the porch; I can see him now. I don't know if he's coming in or going out. I can see his breath. I never saw Jordan's breath once in

the two years we've lived here. Do I mean that I love him?"
She exhaled into the phone.

"Oh, let it be one way or the other," I said. The next
thing I said felt vital. "Tell him it is going down to freezing
tonight. Go, tell him."

Then Nadine told me I was being a romantic—me.

# FEVER

I started out that morning as myself. As steady David Wheelock.

I'd been in my work, and I guess it took me a minute to answer the bell. She had already started to leave, she was walking away by the time I got to the door. I called out to her, "Yes?"

"Dr. Wheelock," she said, turning rapidly. "It's me!"

I nodded, neutrally. Then I said, "Yes," again, too loudly. She was a young woman, maybe twenty-five, lots of makeup, in a long-sleeved beige fitted tunic that flipped out over her black leggings.

"The other day I gave you something that wasn't yours."

I knew the voice. I knew this was a person who sort of did things I asked her to do. There were fewer and fewer such girls around, I even remarked to himself. But I had no idea in the world who she was.

"Uptown Insta Print? Ahnh?" she said. She took a lock of her hair and twisted it with her finger.

"Yes," I said, nodding. "You are the—"

"Over on Maple?"

Our fax machine had broken in the fall. So I had been using the copy shop's. I was writing an as-told-to for a Texas politician, Kleinert. This was the girl I sent the pages through, the one who collected my electronic mail, which was composed almost entirely of insults from Kleinert. The book was a soap job, but the guy wanted whipped cream. It was low work, but I had to do something.

"The other day, I mean right before Christmas, when you came in and I gave you that big stack from Austin? All those? I think I gave you papers of mine, Xeroxes—"

My daughter Charlotte started to wail from her high chair in the kitchen. This went through my mind: *Never leave infant unattended while seated in this device.* I sidestepped rapidly down the hall.

"By mistake," the girl called out, coming in.

I returned with my baby. The girl was standing there, in my foyerless little bungalow. Right inside. I hadn't asked her in.

"A bunch of lyrics. I was with Larry that day, and he's got the group together finally, Desire and the Wannabes. They need a woman vocalist." She took an index finger and stabbed the bony white indentation at the "v" of her dress. My wife Gwen used to call that place between her breasts "my swimming pool," in the long-ago days when she was deprecating about her body. "Me," the girl said, closing her eyes a little longer than needed. "I got my hair done like this."

The only thing I could think to do was to ask her to spell it.

"I look that different hanh?" she said. "Camille, C-A-M-I-L-L-E, A-bare, H-E-B-E-R-T."

I became conscious the baby clothes I'd washed were spilling out of a big basket on the fireplace seat. Charlotte started to squirm in my arms. Camille Hebert followed me down the hall to the kitchen saying, "I was named for the hurricane," and put one of her pastel lacquered fingernails in Charlotte's pink overalls. "The one nobody ever thought would hit Biloxi. Did I tell you that before?" She offered to change the baby, but I said I would do it.

"You are really something, Dr. Wheelock," she said, watching me handle the moist towelettes. I was a good father. I think she saw that, she liked it.

"I'll get the folder," I said, when I had finished taping the new Huggie. I had talked to her, I had. About my work, once, maybe more than once, about being an author. That was the word she used. Author. Then Camille opened her arms and took Charlotte. I didn't even think about it. I handed the baby to her. She didn't think about it either.

I went to my study, a little room beyond the kitchen. This was deep in the house. The wood floors were buckling and there was a leak in the back that was ruining the wallpaper Gwen had put up. She'd done as much of the work as I had, even when she was pregnant. I had always figured there was something agitating my wife at bottom, that she overcompensated. For a long time I thought it was that we couldn't seem to have a child, but we finally did, and that just sped her up, gave her a whole new purpose. Lately she got better at everything she did. For example, she'd recently decided to lose twenty pounds to lower her chances of breast cancer. She just did it, no problem, even though we had moved to New Orleans, where overeating was really worth it. Lately she was leaner when I touched her.

We'd left upstate New York last spring when Gwen got the offer from her law firm here. I had lost my position. That was how we said it, my "position."

Thunderstorms in winter were still strange. In the park that afternoon, I'd been bitten by mosquitos. A voice in me said, there should be snow now. It is actually January. The weather didn't follow any rules. I wasn't accustomed to the South, let me put it that way. I was off my stride. I'm a New Yorker, Brooklyn, actually.

Then it was almost six in the evening and Camille had been sitting in my kitchen for over an hour, poring through several pages of lyrics she'd mixed in with a chapter Kleinert sent back. I was being civil. There had been some lightning, now rain was spraying across the windows.

"Is it cold in here to you?" she asked, finally.

I said no, and asked her if she needed a lift.

"No, I'm fine, maybe I could have a cup of tea? You got a microwave?"

"Camille, I'll have to let you go," I said. I was trying. It didn't work.

"You know what?" she said. "I had this flu last week, was really out of it, it seems like it will kill you."

"I see."

"And I was just fine Saturday, but I'm getting a relapse," she announced, then said nothing for a second. "You notice how people catch everything here? Now they got cholera in the oysters, or they say they do, plus I find out they have a leprosarium on the river." She made a weird bucktooth face, a goofy Charlie Chan.

"Aren't you from here?" I asked her.

"I'm from the prairie," she said. "Not New Orleans."

"The prairie?"

"I'm freezing," she shuddered. "My brother told me it could come back and knock you for one. Right out of nowhere. I guess I better call Larry, huh?"

"I'll take you wherever you want to go," I said. "Who is Larry?" Charlotte was approaching the threshold of the kitchen in her wheeled walker. *Never employ this device near stairs or on uneven surfaces.* Head injury or death may result. "The student infirmary?" I asked, blocking Charlotte's progress. Camille had told me she was taking a few courses at UNO.

"Nothing's open, no dorms, nothing—it's break," she shook her head. Her face darkened then, it was something visible. I assumed she was beginning to understand me. "My sister's ex-husband drove me here when I got the word about the gig. He's halfway to Gulfport by now, the jerk. He came on to me, can you believe it? I mean, I had to get out and hitch." She leaned in the alcove near the phone and dialed. She folded her arm across her waist, so I could have looked at the start of the crease in her bosom, but I chose not to. I thought of her standing on Highway 10, a storm blowing. That road wasn't even built on land, it stood in the midst of the swamp on pillars. There is a twenty-foot drop off the sides, beyond the railing. A person can fall into a swamp.

It crossed my mind, how did I ever forget her name?

"Larry's not there," she said, plopping back into the ash wood chair. Beads of perspiration sprouted out of every pore in her forehead at once. This was breathtaking. You know what that looks like? Like dew.

"You must have a fever," I said to her.

"No lie," she said, rolling her large dark eyes about.

"Can you go to your family?" I asked, directing Charlotte's walker carefully with my foot towards the center of the kitchen.

"Mamou?" she said, wagging her small head with its odd hair. No, no, not beautiful, I corrected myself, made the effort: she looked like a cartoon, a shocked medieval page. She needed shoes that curled up at the toe.

"You came in from Mamou?" Her town was hours away, through the bayous, and past them. I'd read about it. A place where the ethnographers went. She was a real Cajun. So rare. I watched her color fade until she was white as the sink. Charlotte was below, reaching for the black lace cuffs on her legs. Somehow it was a nice moment. I couldn't help that.

"Larry's number has changed. And I have to sing in twenty-four hours," she exclaimed. "I guess I got to be more specific, huh? You have any powders and some oranges?" She said "ah-rahnges."

"Do your parents speak French at home?" I asked. I

hadn't met one before, a Cajun. I was trying to figure out how to make her understand. The South was strange to me. I was curious. The boundaries were hard for me to find, but everybody else knew where they were. To me things were, well, fluid. As in, they ran together, as in, you didn't know how you were being read, or even what you were supposed to be reading.

"You are really a kick, you know that, Dr. Wheelock?" she said as she sat down on one of Gwen's new leather couches. Her tiny pointed hands tore open the fruit I gave her in a single motion.

When I took it I learned her temperature was 103 degrees. I put her under Gwen's afghan. "That's nothing," she said. "People in my family will cook."

She fell fast asleep without any warning, the way my baby did now and then.

"Everybody okay?" Gwen asked when she called.

She was in Fargo taking depositions for a product liability case. She hated to be away. That was what she said.

"Charlotte's doing fine all day," I came back, "but she can't sleep at night, when you are away, you know that."

"I'm really sorry they are keeping me here, that part is agony," she said.

She'd said she'd be away one night. This was her third. She'd done this before. I was imagining her standing there in her thick terry bathrobe, with a little gold chain around her neck. Did that robe have a monogram? Yes it did. The case she was working on was about beauty parlor chairs that snapped a few clients' necks.

"How's the book?" she asked.

"It's in the processor," I said. "Len sent me the new outline. I'll say what they want me to say. Kleinert is a weasel."

"Is it that bad? It's not," Gwen said.

"Never a discouraging word," I said to her.

"Oh, David," she said, disapproving. "How's our girl?"

"She crawled on the rug. She got a mosquito bite, bites, in the park. She gummed some biscuits. She tore around in her walker. She went through a lot of diapers."

"David," she said.

"What?" I said, really wanting her to say what.

Gwen talked mostly, and the more she went on, the more I felt like telling her things weren't going all that well. I was trying to decide how to make this subject apropos. It was okay that she talked, I thought. She was doing something. "Miss you much," I said.

Camille, her color back, her hair flattened, came back into

the kitchen holding a Velvet Underground album I had forgotten I ever owned. She pointed to it in query, mouthing, "Can I play this?"

I said, "Sure, sure, go ahead," aloud.

"Who are you talking to?" Gwen said. "Me?"

"A girl. Camille Hebert."

"We are in the same time, aren't we?" Gwen asked.

"Central."

"What is a girl doing there at seven forty-five at night?"

"She works at the fax place. She gave me some pages that weren't mine. When she came to get them she passed out."

"From what?" Gwen said, a kind of laugh in her voice. "What is this, sweets?"

"She's ill. She has a bug." Camille went back into the other room so I continued. "I can't get her to leave. She's a child. She has nowhere to go. It's awkward."

It was awkward. It was damned awkward.

"Take her to the hospital," Gwen said.

"That's a good idea," I said. "I can't really talk right now. I hear Charlotte." This was a tiny lie. It was either Charlotte or Camille trying to sing.

"Call me tomorrow, huh. Truro Infirmary. Like the blues. It's the closest emergency room to us. The number is by the

phone. I put it there in case—I'll be home Tuesday at eleven
or something. I'm not sure what flight they put me on. I'll
call. This is awful, isn't it?"

"Yes," I said.

*Never look at her narrow nostrils, her mild French girl mustache
while she is sleeping on your couch all night.*

I was feeding Charlotte her instant cereal at seven when
Camille came in, saying, "Thank you so much for that sleep.
Could I take a shower? I saw where the towels are." She
coughed. She sounded horrible. She went on, "Is your wife
here? Does she live here?"

I told her.

"And left you with the little baby?"

"It's the nineties," I said. "We do this."

"I have a boyfriend who was always leaving. Was working
the oil fields until everybody had to leave. I mean Saudi. He
was on every other month, and when he came back, he'd
have this money, a ton of plans, wear me out going places.
Gave me nice high-life albums, though."

"High life?"

"African music," she bit her middle fingernail, a long
one. "Since July he's been living in St. Martinville, building a log house from a thirty-thousand-dollar kit. For us,

he says. But this is all on his menu. You know what I'm saying?"

"I think so," I said. She looked older to me just then. She looked tired.

"You happy, Dr. Wheelock?" Camille asked me. "Over at Uptown we didn't put you in with the happy people."

"Why?" I said.

"When I'd ask you questions about yourself, you'd turn on like a light, for one thing."

"And?"

"Certain people, I pick up on."

"I am, really, I am," I said. "I am." I pointed to my baby, who just then spat up white rice cereal.

I changed Charlotte's clothes. Several days a week I took her to Mrs. Funes, her Nicaraguan sitter, so I could write. I told Camille, who seemed better, coming in after her bath, in a long white T-shirt, pink lace stockings, a white scarf tied around her head so she resembled Civil War wounded, that she could let herself out. I explained to her how to make sure the door was locked.

"I guess I can get a streetcar," she said. She was amusing but somebody ought to tell her, that's what I thought. I had plans. I had work to do. I usually wrote continuously for the first four hours of the day.

"Where are you exactly going?" I asked her.

"I have to sing tonight," she said. "That's why I am in New Orleans," as if this was news to everybody.

"Where?"

"I don't know."

"Well why don't you try Larry then?" I said, grabbing a fork out of Charlotte's tiny fist. *Keep sharp objects out of children's reach.* I lowered my daughter onto the floor, and she started to crawl across the white linoleum towards this houseguest. Uninvited, I guess I'll add. Uninvited houseguest.

She pointed at me the way people mime shooting an arrow. "You got it. I'm going to call his friend Adrian," Camille said.

Maybe she wasn't dumb, but just aesthetic. Or aggressive. This was some Cajun form of aggression. A gris gris. No, I needed the gris gris, to get rid of her, that's what I was thinking. Or a mojo. She would give me the mojo, the spell.

She hung up the phone. Obviously she had made some progress. "I need people who will give me advice. You have any more?"

She wasn't being sarcastic. I found that sweet. She didn't seem to know sarcasm existed.

"Don't take any more powders," I said. "It's aspirin. Your stomach will bleed."

"Yeah?" she said. "I never heard that before. Bleed?"

"Don't take a step," I said, pointing, "the baby, she's by your foot."

"I'm not going to kick her. I'm watching everything. I see what's going on." She took off her scarf, rubbed her temple, reached for the headache powders.

Tell me, then, I almost said. Tell me what's going on. Please be very clear.

Soapy. Fresh coriander, I decided: that was the scent in Mrs. Funes's house. I liked it today, usually I couldn't stand it, I thought as I was driving Camille to the club where she was to practice with the band for a few hours. I was taking a break from Kleinert.

She took up much less room than Gwen, who is five seven and has no ankles. In the early eighties Gwen wore pants, to cover up what she referred to as her piano legs, which were once a secret, something tender between us. When she wore those clothes, I taught at the college near Utica that went broke.

Those were certain days. Those were days in a place that had seasons, like winter summer fall. A place that had rules. I was raised in Brooklyn. In those days in Brooklyn, you didn't go into anyone's house without being invited in a very formal, careful way. You talked on the porch. Everything took place on the porch, in people's driveways, on the sidewalk. Social life, kids playing, I'm talking about.

When I taught at that college, Gwen used to make so much food for faculty dinner parties nobody could eat half of it. Coquilles Saint-Jacques, followed by prime rib. When the place started folding, she would have done anything to keep it going. She was still calling alumni after the trustees had leased the campus buildings to a school for the deaf.

Since we'd moved to New Orleans, she let her legs show. She wore black stockings and short skirts and colors glaring enough to sober up world-famous drunks. A consultant she paid real money to told her to wear these hues.

I liked Magazine but it got a little redundant. There were patches of bad housing, followed by three distinct stretches of galleries and cafes, then a Shoetown, maybe. I couldn't get it. Where I came from you could tell right away if a neighborhood was good or bad, rich or poor, Irish, Italian, or Jewish, etcetera. In New Orleans this is all mixed up. I drove up and down the street several times before I found the place. While I was driving, I remember I felt inordinately sad. I noticed that a clinging, elaborate sadness had been a factor in my life since Charlotte was born, and we'd moved, since Gwen started working so much. Probably for a long time, I'd been attaching large emotions to little things, and feeling neutral about the big things—well, I say this now.

"Hey babes, it's the next-to-last Dixie Beer sign," she said. When she got out I wished her luck.

I felt a little odd then, even stricken, at ten o'clock in the morning on Magazine, to be alone in the car, to be without Camille Hebert. Again I saw her out on that road. I thought perhaps I'd abandoned her—this even though she'd invited herself to my place, this even though she'd barged in on my life, so to speak.

As if I didn't have enough to worry about.

Gwen had been wearing orange, red, popping blue, eye-peeling teal, and taxi yellow, without respite, of late.

This was the first outward sign, as I see it now: when I was supposed to, I didn't call her. I called her two hours later. She answered with a sweet, inquisitory "yes."

"I love you," I said. "I wish you were here."

"Me, too," Gwen answered. Then she was silent.

"What is it?" I said.

"What was going on last night?"

"Nothing, really, she's a singer. She came by to get some pages she'd given me by mistake. Lyrics—"

"Oh, don't tell me anything, just reassure me, okay? No, don't even do that. That would legitimize my asking."

"You can ask," I said.

"How is Charlotte?"

She wouldn't even ask. That struck me. Her discipline. She had more rules than ever, since we'd come to this lapsed sort of town, this southern city.

"She grows every day," I said. "Mrs. Funes swears she's less nervous."

"What do you mean 'less nervous.' Why do you say it that way?"

"What way?"

"David, let's not be like this. It isn't like us," she said softly, quietly. "Is something wrong? Tell me."

In our marriage were many givens, basic definitions. In our marriage, we had always been true. But this time I said, "Like what?"

"You know you can say anything."

"I'm keeping up my end," I said. I don't even know where that came from. Well, I'm not completely sure.

"This is hard too," she said, and then I listened to her recite what she had done the last twenty-four hours. She had a flair for detail. Whiplash at Margie's Hair Skin and Nails. "This never had to happen," she said.

"You believe that?" I asked.

"I believe that," she said. "I even know it. I am certain."

Ladies who leaned back for a blue rinse, in neck braces now for their trouble. I started to laugh. I did. I started to laugh.

"Do you think I am having fun?" Gwen said.

"I don't think you are having ordinary kind of fun," I said. There was a time when I adored her for throwing herself into things because it was obvious she had to. I always marveled. I thought about the old uncompromising New York winters, about the gallons of hot soup she made when she was a gung-ho wife. How she always used to ask, how is it? Do you like it?

"That's not where we are," she said. "I know it isn't. I just know it. You are just down."

"So?" I said, hearing in my own voice a certain invading zest.

That day, Charlotte didn't nap for Mrs. Funes, and then, when she got home, she was too wound up to fall asleep. I had to strap her in the Snugli and pace for hours. She wailed when I touched her, wailed when I let her alone. I didn't sleep at all, really, I just catnapped in the leather recliner while she fussed on my breast. The next day Kleinert woke me at eight, to tell me my prose was "shot full of holes. Is there something wrong with you? Don't you tape it when I tell you my story?"

Let me explain Kleinert's life: greed, boosterism, and impenetrable megalomania bred in sandy Waco. He goes on: "Can't you fill in with a little snazz? Have you ever been introduced to finesse? Why is the thing such a downer? You have a problem? Can't you stretch out the high spots?"

Charlotte was fast asleep when I gave her to Mrs. Funes, which meant she had gotten her days and nights "mixed up." This was a tendency I had gone to great lengths to set right months before.

Most of the day I napped, then I tried to work, but my eyes hurt me awfully. I couldn't even look at the screen. Charlotte was wide awake when I picked her up, not a good sign. I had a few beers while she was practicing her creeping. Early that evening she picked up a white scarf off the floor and handed it to her daddy, I mean, to me.

*Never start car without securing your infant in the restraint system*—that's what I was thinking.

But it was midnight and I thought the top of my head might float right off. I was driving down Magazine wearing Charlotte in a Snugli pouch underneath my gray windbreaker. In the infant seat beside us was the scarf and a brown paper bag from an all-night Walgreen's. When I zipped the windbreaker up in front, I had a big belly, a real gut.

The place was only a quarter full, and Camille was sitting alone in the corner with a piano singing "Fever." She did this rather bravely, considering she wasn't in good voice. I wondered if it was just the flu.

The bartender was a heavy man with a T-shirt that read, "Boogie 'Til You Die." I was compelled to point to the downy head under my chin—but the man only shrugged.

Everything I saw, I heard a little voice saying, yes, yes, that too, yes, that, and why not. I was fighting this voice.

"Dr. Wheelock," she said, as if she had been expecting me, "how you-all are? Larry was dreaming. One guy showed up. So I asked for the piano, this old thing in the back. It was in tune. You know how unusual that is? This city is underwater. You generally have to tune a piano every two weeks."

"You mean below sea level?" I said, waiting to get the order to leave. Of course I was going to go. I didn't even have to reenforce this idea. *From myself* I would get the order to go. It was coming. I was waiting.

"My little sweetie in there?" She touched Charlotte's head with her small good-looking hand.

"This is for you," I said, "and you left this at my house."

She made the Charlie Chan face again and I remembered what it had looked like to me the first time she did it. This time it was charming, proof I was drunk, I thought, or worse.

She took the scarf and the paper bag. The Valentine's display had just gone up in the drugstore. I'd bought a five-pound heart of Pangburn's Chocolates. In the bag as well were two bottles of blue cold medicine. The labels read "No aspirin." These were small acts, at the time, spontaneous, unpremeditated. That's how I saw them.

"I have been thinking you should look out for yourself, huh? You could be getting it. Larry's supposed to come here. He's taking me to Opelousas in the morning. Wants to make up for the fiasco. It's not what you think, though," she said.

I realized I had no idea what she thought I thought.

"Larry's gay," she said.

Then I knew.

I hopped off the stool. I had to grab the edge of the bar with both hands. I was losing my balance, mostly because of the weight of my baby in the front, but this seemed desirable. I paused, not yet poised. I really didn't know what next. I had absolutely no plan, no projection, no outlook.

Yet, I felt great. There is something here, in this story, about intention and prevention, and rules and being alive, being fluid, but I haven't worked it all out completely yet.

I've had too much else to deal with. Camille steadied me. I leaned forward and kissed her for this.

"Now, I've got feelings for you, Dr. Wheelock," she whispered, thickly sighing, as we started, "but I got to tell you it still hurts to breathe."

I thought this was very funny, this remark. Wasn't this funny, that she said it hurt to breathe. So did she. So did Camille.

I reached around her the way I might reach around Gwen, but there was so much less of her than there had ever been of my wife. My hands could find out so much in so little time. She had a tiny Braque collage of a body, a little cubist guitar, full of angles. Nothing, nothing at all, was where it was supposed to be.

Making out, leaning sideways on the bar, was a struggle. We had to devise a one-armed operation, like the sidestroke, alternating left and right, the kind lifesavers use in deep water. Charlotte squirmed between us, vital and fat. Camille's kisses were exactly what I had always wanted kisses to be: uncanny, how this was so.

At home, under my down comforter, the delight took over entirely, the deliciousness, the ease. I had forgotten what it was like to be desired in that way, to be convinced you are someone's elixir.

When she finally slept, her breath caught, faintly, in her chest. I loved this sound—muffled waters.

In the morning, on the way back from Mrs. Funes's house, I unrolled my Toyota windows. I kept telling myself to think about the night, what a horrendous thing had happened, but even though I wanted to, my mind kept following off down other paths. Nature was one. Half the trees on the streets were blooming and the other half were laden with dying, purplish leaves. The camellia bushes in the neighborhood were still going. Below them were puddles of pink blooms turning brown. In Louisiana everything was simultaneous. Nothing was chopped into seasons. Now I saw. A certain convergence of opposites. There was a mist so fine it was possible to inhale it, or maybe you just let it flow into your pores. Underwater. There was a way in which feeling bad, even hating myself a little, felt perfectly marvelous—was this something you could even say to another person? It doesn't make sense, does it, when I say it here. I was terribly aware of the beauty of the broken-down storefronts and houses, of the imperfect places, of the wounded, the flawed, the ugly, the never-very-good.

I think I even asked myself at this point, *what are you*

*turning into?* But I had the feeling that answer would be delayed.

"Gwen called," Camille said. "That's your wife, isn't it?" She was sitting in the kitchen in a tiny yellow dress that looked to me like a nightgown, but it was obvious she thought she was dressed.

"You answered?" I said, alarmed. "What?"

"She said she'd be in at eleven-twelve. Delta. At the airport."

I just looked at her. "Go," I said.

"I said I was the maid," she said, nodding.

What maid? She was going, of course. I told her to go. I heard her getting her things together. In seconds I picked up in the kitchen, the bedroom, the other bedroom, the hall. I stripped the sheets off. But my head pounded. I was sick. I found all the small, dangerous toys. *Never leave small objects within infant's reach. Choking or strangulation may result.* I fixed myself some quick tea. *Never use metal utensils in the microwave. Never take four aspirin on an empty stomach.*

"Go!" I told her, when I saw her in the hall, in the bathroom. She was everywhere, suddenly, I couldn't get away from her.

Next thing, Mrs. Funes called, to say Charlotte was vomiting. She had a fever. I called the pediatrician, but I couldn't get through. Four times. The fifth time I picked up, there was no dial tone. It was Gwen, calling back, on the line.

"It didn't ring," she said.

"I'm psychic," I said.

"I'll just get a cab," she said. "I'm early. The plane landed early. You hired a maid?"

"What? No. Not a maid. Darling. Darling."

"Soon," Gwen said.

I piled Camille's things on the porch, handed her a stray Guess T-shirt. I had already said good-bye twice. But she was still sitting in the Adirondack porch chair under the stucco arch when I came outside on my way to retrieve Charlotte.

"Go," I said. "I'm sorry. I'm so sorry."

"I am too," she said with her interesting mouth. "I know. I get it."

"I mean it," I said. "When I say 'go' do you hear another word?" I meant this. I had serious doubts. This business about how I was being read. This was exactly what I was thinking. I wasn't angry, really. I didn't want her to ever go, actually.

"Sure," Camille said. "I'm going, okay? I'm going."

"I have to get the baby. She's coming down with something. I'll drop you off anywhere."

"No, no," she said, "there's a streetcar," with a certain kindness, "I GET IT," picking up herself and her things, and swinging her arms as she walked away down the street, like a young Audrey Hepburn rather, I thought. Good-bye, good-bye, I said under my breath. Better of course, if she were to leave. Better, of course. For her. Better. I was perfectly willing to say forever good-bye at that exact point, I think.

A little later I wondered if I had the same body as I had yesterday, the way this one hurt at every joint. Charlotte was hot when I got her. She fell fast asleep in the car.

When I drove up back at the house, Gwen was standing on the sidewalk with her suitcase that had wheels. Camille Hebert was in front of her, holding the box of chocolates, opened. Gwen had raised one hand the way Indians in old movies say how.

"What is this? Some kind of joke? David? Who are you? Are you David?" she said, pivoting around when I walked up. "Please tell me."

"This is a big mistake. This is Camille. She just came by—"

"Yes," Gwen said, waiting, expectant.

"I thought you had gone," I told Camille. "There was a streetcar, no?"

"I was going," Camille said, "but then I saw her—"

"Why does she call me 'her' like that?" Gwen asked, her eyes going to me. "Tell me right now."

Camille turned to Gwen, "Your baby is sick. She has the flu. It is going around. David too. Everybody here is coming down with something."

"How do you know?" Gwen said.

"I know, I know plenty," Camille said, popping a milk-chocolate-covered caramel in her mouth.

"The baby's sick? How sick? How could this happen?" Gwen stood there for a second, no words coming, in her impeccable red jacket, her chevron design pocket square. "This can't happen."

"It does," I think I sort of enjoyed saying. "It did. It does. It did."

Turning to get the baby out of the car, I found myself touching Camille's soft cheek. I didn't intend to do this in the way I intended customary things. It felt unpreventable. But of course, it was the awful breach. All things were set in stone, everything became perfectly clear, there was a straight line between all the events of the last three days, perfect cause and effect, the second I touched Camille's cheek. Behind me, waiting, was Gwen. All this time, I was breaking down, a perfect wreck, somehow I knew this, but I went forward, as if I were single-minded, as if I knew what the hell I was doing. That is what is asked of people, isn't it. That they know what the hell they are doing. It is a great deal to ask, I think now. I was running a fever at the time.

In this awful moment I somehow turned to philosophy. I had lots I wanted to say to Gwen, actually, but all that came out was, "It does, it did." This was incredibly stupid. I know that now. I meant to say much wiser things.

One of the aspects of this whole mess that strikes me lately—how I am outside it, watching so often, how I've started now to see everything coming, from both women, no surprises, when before I was totally unprepared. Very often it's as if I'm watching a character with whom I identify mildly, and when another awful thing is about to happen to him I groan in anticipation, I double over at the outrageous complications, at the melodrama, how terribly he's screwed up, but it doesn't always faze me that it's me: I don't feel it yet that way. I don't have that defining grief. I wonder sometimes when that recognition will come, that waking up. I even long for it. This distance, this sense of philosophy, began the second I touched Camille's cheek.

I wanted to tell Gwen then, "Don't you know we are lived as much as we live, we are driven as much as we drive? You can't prevent everything, darling, darling. There are things nobody can see coming."

She would have probably repeated herself, she was livid, not thoughtful, exactly. I don't blame her. This is what she keeps saying to me now: who are you? in her New York accent, are you David? How am I supposed to talk to you when I don't know who you are?

# GAUGUIN

When people ask him about it, Paul still says it's mysterious to him. He knows he could start back when David Duke was running for Governor of Louisiana. But if someone wants to hear the story, he usually begins with a man in limbo, himself—dusk on a Monday, late in August 1992. He was driving downtown to his office for some files he wanted to look over before he left. He was flying to Wellfleet in forty-odd hours. Meredith would be there. He looked up and saw the overpass: Interstate 10 West a parking lot. He thought, tank-truck turnover, jackknife, petrochemical spill. Bopal. He turned on the local news radio, got the headline, "Coming Up: Mayor Sidney Barthelme on the Evacuation of New Orleans."

He turned around in the road, went back to his little rent house on St. Helena, to wait and see, which would describe his whole life in Baton Rouge at that time—he was waiting and seeing.

The year before when David Duke hit, when he got in the runoff for governor, Meredith called him out of the blue, from Boston. She wanted to know what Paul was going to do. They'd been friends in law school, but involved with other people. Somebody in her new firm told her to call, say, "Stay down there like Nadine Gordimer." But Meredith didn't think so. They went on to other subjects. This developed.

As a matter of fact, that same Duke afternoon, Diana Landry from across the street came over with her son A. J. She was wearing a "Vote for the Crook, It's Important" T-shirt. "Saw your No-Nazis Sticker," she said. Paul assumed he was going to be fired however things turned out. Buddy Roemer, the governor, who hired him through Harvard connections, was out of the mansion in any case. Paul was a lawyer in the Department of Environmental Quality. He'd already made some calls—a friend in Princeton told him about a job in Albany. He was trying.

"Leave, everybody should," she said. "If you aren't from here. I am so ashamed of this place." Then she paused. "But if you want to join the underground I know where to start." Next, she was yelling at her son, who was climbing a delicate

crepe myrtle bush. "You can call me. We'll get that sucker."
He did join her. There were some crazy weeks that fall.

Now, this limbo Monday, in August, almost a year later,
things with Meredith had gotten more interesting. Paul had
not been laid off after the new governor was inaugurated.
Nobody understood this. Paul just assumed it was a matter
of time. Meredith was handing his resume around to insti-
tutes on Route 128. It was her cause, others had taken it up
as well: getting him back to New England. Although Paul
was a stoical young man, rather tall, who could be riled but
not easily, he was quietly beginning to panic. He hadn't actually been with Meredith *in person* in all this time. But one
thing that kept him going was that he and Meredith were
closer and closer, by Internet.

When he got home, his trip to the office denied him, the
phone rang. Diana across the street. "We've got some D batteries," she said and he wondered who "we" was, since she
told him one morning when he was jogging that she and her
husband Virgil (Cajun, ropey arms, a sculptor) split up in the
early spring. Otherwise, he hadn't spoken to her for months.
"What kind of radio do you have?"

"Huh?" he said. "What's going on in New Orleans?"

"Andrew," she said.

He hadn't been watching TV lately. "Who?"

"After Betsy, we didn't have power for five days."

"I'm going to Wellfleet," he said.

"Where?" Diana said.

"Why are they evacuating New Orleans?"

"Not yet, maybe some early birds," she said. "The hurricane's got them going." He remembered she was a chatterer. To be nice he suppressed his love of the point.

First thing in the morning, Meredith called. He was thrilled. Raised in Newton, she still dropped her r's—he'd almost forgotten. She was at the Cape already, no modem, so they had to use their voices.

"Twenty feet of water in New Orleans," she said.

"There's no water in New Orleans," he said.

"But there will be—"

"No," he said. "This place has a specialty in threatened disasters."

"It's if the locks break, there will be. Do you have them where you are?" she said.

He was interested in her tone. All this time, it had been maybe only chummy. He couldn't tell. The Net is not a hot medium, instead disembodied, like conversations in the afterlife.

"There's a whole Gulf Coast, a thousand-mile stretch where it could hit," he said.

"How do people stand it?" she said. "Waiting, not knowing?"

He didn't have an answer. Call waiting beeped. Because of the time, he decided he'd better take it. It was his boss, Fletcher L'Enfant. Meredith said, "Go ahead, you work for him—I'll call back," before he could tell her L'Enfant could be ignored.

"Son, don't go to work today."

Even if he was waiting for it, it was a creepy feeling, being canned at seven-fifty in the morning. He sat down. L'Enfant called him son. Paul was turning thirty-one. "Nonessential state employees. Just got the call. The hurricane."

He didn't feel relieved. "Will somebody let me in? So I can get that Filtrum Reprocessing file?"

"No," he said in that over-slow voice he used when he thought Paul didn't follow, "closed up, zippo."

"But I'm on my way out of town!" He imagined L'Enfant was trying to keep him from recommending fines for that plant, and being exquisitely nice about it.

"Fill your bathtub," L'Enfant said. "You'll be fine. Bye bye."

When he hung up, the phone rang almost immediately. Meredith.

After describing his conversation with L'Enfant, he asked

her, to entertain her, "What good does a bath do in a hurricane?"

"That would never happen in Boston. Your boss would never tell you to fill your tub." She was giggling. Phone was so sensual. "Oh, Albertine is desperate to make a call. Ciao."

About nine-thirty that same morning he was in a hardware store on Perkins Road. The atmosphere was snappy. People were out around town, on a mass scavenger hunt. He told himself the best way to make the sun shine in this situation—not that he cared really, since he was on his way out—was to have an ample umbrella. So he was standing in front of a bin full of picked-over supplies—pen lights, busted kerosene lanterns, taped bundles of linty wicks. A woman came up to give him advice—the Radio Shack was having a delivery at 10:30, the D batteries at one chain mart were out of date. And then on to dry ice, how Hurricane Betsy barreled up the Mississippi gaining strength. He couldn't get this woman to stop. He remembered an article he read once, about the southern urge to explain. It didn't explain.

The first day he went out to the market after Duke was in the runoff, a complete stranger, just like this lady, a frank woman in an all-weather coat, the creased upper lip of a smoker, came up to him—"Can you believe it? The Saints are going to pull out. We won't get the Olympic trials . . .

Used to tell people he was going to burn his mother's bed.
She was an alcoholic."

"Who was an alcoholic?" he asked.

"His mamma. And his daddy—don't believe any of that
Laotian stuff."

"Laotian stuff?"

"That he was in Laos with his daddy working for the CIA.
S'crazy." She touched his sleeve.

"Who?"

"Who else? The Antichrist. I can't sleep. Can you?" She
progressed with him to the cash register. "What can we do?"

He told her about the underground Diana had led him to.
A bunch of them, meeting down at an office suite on a boulevard in the deep suburbs. They were using this law firm's
seventeen telephones, and a set of disks somebody had stolen
from the party headquarters, to reach every Republican in
the Parish. Over the first week, all kinds of people showed
up: little Jewish ladies, professors from everywhere, kids, old
ministers, Italian lawyers, arty friends of Diana's, even her
brother Danny, a deputy sheriff. They couldn't park at the
complex itself—had to use the back of a Circle K across the
street. A secretary let them in, by a side door. There was
a password. After this got underway, the hard core of the
group—somehow Paul was involved—started pressuring

politicians and coaches to speak in public, talking rich people into running ads about Duke's past, haranguing the stations every time a reporter let Duke off the hook. Didn't do anything else for three weeks. Paul got so wrapped up in it he never even called that guy in Albany back. He lost weight. Ran a fever. Meredith's message on the Net: "It's existential. You are a partisan." Smiley.

He wrote back, "Get me out of here."

This Tuesday morning, Andrew still pending, he extricated himself from this lady. His booty: two cheap flashlights, sixteen C batteries, a huge expensive cooler.

As he was driving home past massive oaks, palmettos, big banana trees, it occurred to him all he had to do, of course, was change his ticket. So he went in and dialed, and waited a million years, feeling like a fool, for the Delta operator. He recognized he was losing his edge, down in Louisiana.

While he floated in the crackling phone noise, he saw Cape Cod, the horizon there, so even and free of business, pines, grey and blue. He thought of Thoreau. How Yankee he was. Finally the operator came on: no seats out of New Orleans or Baton Rouge.

In this North he saw, the laws of cause and effect were well established. Meredith and himself because they've always liked each other, it made sense. These rules didn't work in Louisiana. Duke, for example, was not entirely a horrible event in the lives of his many enemies. Even specific irony didn't apply often enough in this place. For example, Paul was prepared, in a matter of speaking, for the hurricane by this time, which should have meant it wouldn't come within a thousand miles. This would work anywhere north of Baltimore.

St. Helena was Mexican slang for blondes, he was thinking as he watched Mrs. Diana Landry crossing the street in front of his house. He cringed a little. Then he remembered he'd tell her that he'd heard that David, politically dead, was taking the insurance exam. Her crinkly light hair in the breeze.

"They have dry ice at Party Time," she said. "You want me to pick you up some?" She was wearing tight floral leggings—wisteria growing on her legs. A. J. was behind her, pulling a red wagon loaded with baseball equipment across the lawn. "Virgil came over and boarded up the house—just left," she said, sounding pissed. From the doorway he could see her place—the old failing oak in the front yard, the mustard-yellow plywood slapped up on all the windows. "I'm sorry to have to ask, but you got a beer?" she said. This was the most personal she'd been in ten months.

He had things called Turbo Dogs, which were beers, in the refrigerator. She had one, he didn't. She went on to say that at Party Time, you had to stand in line. Then she returned to the subject of Virgil. "He wants to see we're okay, okay," she said, biting her lip. "I say like, 'Okay 'til you showed up,'" one side of her mouth drawn up. He wondered if she knew what that did to her face. "Don't look at me like that," she said, her lips going instantly back to a pout. Her manic skittishness should have bothered him more.

Suddenly she announced, "Mike Graham's on." She pulled a big tracking map she got free at a drugstore out of her jeans pocket. They both thought A. J. was in the dark little back room where Paul hid his television, but when they got there, they found he wasn't. Diana picked up Paul's remote.

The weatherman said, "Landfall by late Wednesday. Warnings from Pascagoula to Lake Charles—" They heard glass breaking. Running to the front of the house, they found A. J. putting out the small panes along the side of the front door. With his baseball bat. When he opened the door to ask A. J. what he thought he was doing, Paul noticed the air, still and thick. The entire neighborhood—the little cottages, the huge old live oaks, the lampposts and slate walks—was floating inside a glass of buttermilk. Diana came out and yanked her son inside.

"What's wrong with him?" Paul asked her, sounding more upset than he felt inside—it was this limbo.

She was almost Paul's height, her eyes large. She said, "They don't know. Or won't tell me." He realized this bold, sort of bloated face she had now was the way she looked right before she cried.

She went into his bathroom with A. J., who had nicked his finger on a piece of glass. "I didn't mean—" Paul said. She looked at him as if he knew everything. Then he rushed off to his study for cardboard, filmy brown packing tape. He came back to the front saying, "I can fix it," but when he got there, his broom was leaning against the foyer wall, his front door was closed and locked. Through the broken panes, he could see Diana and A. J. bounding across the street. He felt terrible.

At three, Paul decided to dismiss the thought of Andrew entirely. He was trying to figure out if any dry cleaners would do his things by morning. Then, when he wandered back into the den, the TV was still on, but someone had pressed the mute. There was a computer enhancement of the storm. It covered the gulf, from Florida on the right side of the screen to the tops of the islands south of New Orleans on the left. For a second it came right up off the map, and out of the box. It startled him. He stared. It was like God, or that stuff at the end of *Raiders of the Lost Ark.* The next second, he saw a sign on a boarded-up building in New Orleans, "ANDREW TAKE IT OUT ON FERGIE." He laughed, actually very hard, for someone alone. He watched the Baton Rouge commercials, in despair. Monster truck rallies, half-naked Heather who wants you at the Gun and Knife Show. He wondered what was playing at the American Repertory Theatre. He took a snatch of a nap, woke to banging.

Diana, on his front stoop in a plastic poncho. It was late in the afternoon, getting strange. She was holding a narrow piece of plywood over the place where A. J. put out the window. She had a hammer and nails.

"Hey, I rent, don't worry about it," he said coming out.

"No. I'm so sorry," she said. "I left A. J. on the Nintendo. Maybe I do that too much." She handed him a picnic thermos, huge. "I brought you hurricanes."

He was grateful. Once before he got drunk with her. The night Duke lost. She recited a ditty to him, the Cajun consider-the-lilies-of-the-field, "Look at the birds in the yard/ who feeds 'em cher." He remembered this right now. A still drizzle, outside. The buttermilk leaving condensation. That big silent swirling thing he saw on TV, he thought of telling her about it, someone here, who wouldn't think he was crazy, Meredith would, but instead he said, "There's a thousand places it could come in," because he was shy.

"Mike's moved landfall way up," she said. "It's coming in at Vermilion Bay or maybe Morgan City."

In Morgan City the children had some terrible brain cancer. Statistically significant. A lot of people blame the toxic waste processor there. He had been on it for seven months. In fact, in June a guy from Hartford told him about an opening at his firm, but Paul was in Morgan City so much he missed the deadline.

"Winds are still at one-fifty," she said. "The eyewall will be here by midnight."

*Eyewall.* How fluent she was. He said, "It will fizzle."

"You still going?" she asked.

"Yea."

"Getting outta here, huh?" jutting her lower chin a little bit as if to mimic some matter-of-factness that was generally Paul's and not hers. Suddenly he wondered if she wanted him to go. If she had an opinion about it. This came up, out of nowhere. For a second those big un-dangerous dunes at the Cape spun out into space, and he was just in the present with Diana, in the middle of this late, odd afternoon. He felt a little stunned. Maybe she saw this. "Yea, uh-huh," she said, now nodding to mock him—wasn't he a lucky duck, wasn't he? But he had to do his packing. He had shirts to wash. "Don't you know to fill your tub?" she said—taking off for his bathroom.

"Why's this in here?" she called to him when he got there. "I swear Paul, you got to get square with your TV, boy." She handed him his remote, which she'd dropped beside the tub herself, some time ago. In several ways, an unstandable woman, he reminded himself.

He stood in the doorway trying to celebrate when she finally left. He noticed breaths, little explosions of rain, under the light on their street, which had come on early. It was an idiosyncratic rain. Usually you could count on rain to be fairly uniform, he was thinking.

He did a damn good job—toothbrush, Mitchum, Vidal Sassoon, the works. All in a little nylon Lands End bag, zipped up, with room to spare. He finished washing and laid out his outfits, even ironed a few shirts—he'd given up on the idea of finding a cleaners. Lined up his socks. He didn't forget the Eternity cologne, the rugged cotton sweaters he never got a chance to wear because Louisiana was too hot. This took time. At ten he watched the local news, which he hadn't done since the Duke campaign. Back then the news made him sick—the reporters milked the story for all it was worth, at the same time they behaved like cowards, he thought. National news was even worse, completely clueless, missed all the ironies. But tonight the local reporters were standing in outrageously windy spots, their cheeks so wet with violent rain, they seemed to be weeping. He suddenly felt he knew them very well, could go into their hearts if necessary. Some had already been told to evacuate, they said, as they wobbled all over the screen. One guy he called a fascist the year before was standing in the middle of tall, violently swaying cane. The scale was off. He was a grasshopper, reporting from a very unruly lawn. "Chances are high it will hit here," he said. A foray into the obvious. Paul felt for this guy, his high eyebrows, syrupy Cajun eyes. He wanted to go into the TV to say, "Pierre, get in the van, it's going to blow."

Thank God he was headed for Wellfleet.

Then there was a live report from the Hurricane Center in Coral Gables. The director had been up for days. The center itself was hit. Some on his crew were electrocuted. He was slovenly, incoherent. Paul was well into Diana's concoction by then. It tasted like Hawaiian punch plus grain alcohol, and he was meditating on the word "here." He called Meredith.

"Oh, Jesus, are you anywhere near La Place?" she asked.

Once again he was thrilled with the sound of her voice. It was throaty. "There was a tornado," she said. "Can you go to a shelter?" just as he saw the red bulletin flash across his screen.

"I'm fine," he said. "That's over near New Orleans."

"I think it's headed right there," she said.

"Hell or high water, really," he said, "the plane's tomorrow, three-thirty."

"We're all worried about you," she said. "Albertine says when she heard you'd gone to Louisiana it was like that painter who went to Tahiti, that's what she thought of."

Albertine was a woman they went to law school with. From Smith. Her eyes were magnified by her glasses. "She and Russell came out, remember Russell?" Meredith said. "We were all so worried. Glued to the Weather Channel," she waited. "Paul? You there?"

"What? Yea," he said. "I'm not there, I'm here."

"Well, yes. I know where you are."

"Here," he said. "It's different."

"I know," she said, "tell me."

"It's insoluble," he said. "Isn't it?"

"I don't think so," she said. "Here is there for you and there for me is here for you," her deep laugh. "For now."

"Yes it is, it is, but not really," he said.

Meredith insisted it was. She repeated herself. She was flirting, he knew, but he was having difficulty responding. He was serious about all this; he wasn't sure at all why.

After they finally said goodnight, he decided to sleep in the back den, which had only one window, and that one shaded by heavy wooden jalousies. He bedded down in front of the TV, under a thin blanket. His flight bag was propped up on his little black couch. He had finished off the jug. And this was all very native, he thought, to be drunk on sweet drinks and be alone, listening to the wind hurling through the banana trees. I really must go, he thought. Really.

At one of the desolate hours, three or four in the morning, he ventured into the kitchen. Cotton mouth. Reaching toward the left, he touched the light switch.

No light. None in the fridge.

In the dark, while he drank all the orange juice from the carton, he thought of the normal-size sky they have up there on the Cape, to try and calm down. He saw himself and Meredith McCartel, a Unitarian, going along the beach, having a thoughtful conversation. He knew peace of mind. He knew exactly what came after that afternoon's walk. He prayed he hadn't upset her.

He staggered back to bed, which was the floor.

When he got up again, the kitchen was filled with a strange pink light. He assumed it was morning. The pecan tree outside his window was waving at the base of its trunk, a big timid hula girl. He put his good French roast beans into the grinder—no whir.

For a long time he sat at his little metal table in an old tubular chair, and watched this tree and the others dance. He listened. Around eight his house started to groan. Then all the trees were swaying back and forth, like backup singers. It was positively choral—the tops in one direction, the bottoms in another. Of course this was terrible, but that didn't keep it from being interesting. Around nine he heard the whistle, like he was on a ship. Andrew going through the lamp that hung from his little porch. His ears were aching by this time. He was surprised when the phone rang.

"I got through!" Meredith said, triumphantly. "How's your airport?" she said. He was thinking about a tree across the street, in Diana's front yard, how heavy it was.

"I don't know," he said. He hadn't called.

"I'll call," she said. "Are you Delta?"

"It's very bad, here," he said. "My ears."

"According to the Weather Channel, it's to your west."

He didn't answer.

"Are you okay?" she said—this irritation, now. "You sounded sort of—"

"I'm fine," he said.

"I don't know, were you drinking last night?"

"Drinking?" This was out of character for him, that he would lie to someone that way.

"I'll call," she said. "Delta." She said it firmly. "How can you stand it. Don't you just wish you knew exactly how this was going to turn out? I'd go crazy."

He agreed he couldn't stand it, of course, but later when he recalled this, he recognized some reservations, which he hadn't uttered. What he said was, "My ears are splitting open." The barometric pressure.

"Last night they said it might fly by and only land in Mobile, how far is that?"

"Mobile?" he asked. "I think it's here."

"I mean your plane," she said.

"I'm too close to the window," he said.

"Oh Paul don't," she said. "How bad can it be?"

"It's a hurricane, Meredith," he said. "It really doesn't matter what they say on cable. I'm so sorry, I really am," and he was, but then he hung up. Next, he was crawling across the floor. As if, if he were to stand up he might be showing the present some disrespect. As if he had seen things, been shown signs. He headed toward the front of the house, though it would have been safer to stop in the little hallway next to the den. He wanted a view of the whole street. When he got there, he saw that the several enormous live oaks on St. Helena looked like giants buried in the sand, their heads poking up, straining to get out. The root systems, their shoulders, pulled up more soil with every heavy gust. The trees were heaving. It was amazing. He gazed over at Diana's house, blank, eyeless, the thick plywood patches.

The night Duke lost the race, he could see the candlelight in her windows from his living room. She used little votives for the party. That way she wouldn't have to really clean, she joked. Her home life was not the best right then. For the three weeks of the runoff, they were arguing—Virgil said she was gone too much, and he wanted to know how she could support Edwards no matter who his opponent was. A lot of couples had split over the election. At the party there was a pool, you could pick the point spread. By that time most people figured Edwards had been bound to win all along—he'd never been in real danger. The underground might have felt used, and bitter. That would have made sense, Paul thought. Instead everybody danced to Neville Brothers, Doctor John, Zydeco, a little Dewey Balfa. There were Creoles there, lawyers and other rich men, with paunches. The journalists who listened to some of them had all kinds of stuff they couldn't print, crimes of Duke, rumors about Edwards. There were professors from Southern University, and a tall woman from Sri Lanka, a physicist, with her husband, Buddhists, a man raised in Hungary, who'd been in the resistance in the war. They had all worked at the phone bank one night or another, but it was sort of amazing to see them there together at once, come from so many different realms, chomping on corn chips. Duke's losing was a certainty, they said they'd never had a question. But at the end of the evening, when it came to how the precincts voted, parish by parish, people from Louisiana went up to the screen, asked for silence. If Duke was defeated in their home precinct, they shouted, "All right!" and held their fists in the air, hugged people. Everybody cried and asked each other personal questions. Where were you from, really, where were you going if Duke had won. When she was in the middle of a long complaint, Paul asked Diana why she ever wanted to marry Virgil. She looked at him—actually very pretty to him just then, another man's wife, and that was okay, that was the mood, no secrets, no status. She said, "Does what you want have much to do with how your life plays out? I think very little." And then she grinned, like it was all right with her, what she'd just said. At the time he thought her remark incredibly strange. He had not forgotten this completely by the day of the hurricane.

Just then the huge oak in her yard succeeded in liberating itself from the soil. A thundering cracking sound. The entire root system toppled out, taking up half the lawn with it. It fell towards her house. In the center of the mass of roots now visible, a black hole ran through. Dead all along. He couldn't see her roofline any more. He crawled to his front door, stood, and opened it up.

Actually, when he unlocked it, it opened itself.

The wind was primary, sovereign. Music, playing at different speeds, different intensities. The rain was being thrown out in gasps, violently, then breathily. As if the wind had to reach inside of itself periodically to find more water to throw forth. Smaller trees, twice as tall as himself, bent down to the ground, then snapped back up, over and over. The street was a river. From his porch he could see that her carport and part of her roof was crushed. He imagined Diana and A. J. trapped inside. Then Paul's nerves were a golden web, lighting him up inside his arms, his thighs, his neck.

He made it across—he was blown, really, that's how it looked, or he was picked up by an invisible hand. He touched down on the little concrete disks that made the path to her front door. He was imagining how he'd break in.

He pounded on the door, stood outside and waited. Never once did he think he was stupid. The door cracked open. There she was. She was fine.

"You crazy? You out of your mind?" She had him in.

It reminded him of a lake at night, inside—so dark with the windows boarded, the light from kerosene lamps. She had shiny oak floors, with puddles here and there. Water was running in underneath the bedroom doors along the hallway on the side of the house where the roof was damaged. There were towels and cotton blankets tossed around, used recently to swab the floors, he supposed, then abandoned. When he looked back to Diana, he saw she was holding a fan of playing cards in her hand, sitting on her skirted, winged old couch in a long cotton nightgown. She looked flushed, younger. Her calves were very white, and smooth, and in places dappled pink, and she had big work boots on, her husband's old ones, he guessed. A. J., beside her, was also holding some cards, and eating caramel corn from a pottery bowl, dark blue. The boy, who had a ruddy complexion and mousey blond hair, looked strangely cherubic in this light. From a cooler, dry ice mist furled towards them.

"D'you run across in your bare feet like that?" she said. "That's so wild."

"I saw the tree fall."

A. J. was shuffling the cards. He was excellent at this, very smooth, didn't drop one, Paul noticed.

"Did you hear that?" she asked her son, beaming. A. J. was very calm. The hurricane pacified him. "It gave us a scare, but we just sat tight." Paul took a seat on an ottoman, on a damp blanket. They dealt him in. He won a few, but mostly he lost to Diana and A. J. She cheated so her son would win. Generally, he'd say that was a bad idea, but right then he found it endearing. They ate crawfish salad cold from the dry ice, and delicious. Some boudin. He felt as if he'd been there forever, listening to the storm slowly dying down. More than once it occurred to him the house was going to collapse; this made him enjoy the moment more somehow.

A. J. went into the kitchen at one point. When they were alone, Diana looked at Paul with her wide-apart eyes, and reached toward his jaw as if to check his shaving, or to bring his face toward her, or to make sure he was real—the place didn't look real at all, stage smoke creeping along the floor. He leaned forward to hear what she was going to say, or maybe to do, attracted by her lovely attention. It was strange, how calm this all made him. But then she said, "Weren't you the one who was going somewhere?"

And when he tells this story he always jumps a little ahead, at this point, to that walk they took. It was about two-thirty, and the winds had died down and he and Diana and A. J. ventured out into her wrecked yard. Paul was carrying his flight bag. The airport was open. Down St. Helena, almost every tree was down or damaged. Things that were hidden before, he noticed, were exposed now by the winds—the flashy white wood inside old branches, the underside of the leaves, all silver. Immaculate was the word that came to mind. They passed many women, their neighbors, standing on their porches, their front doors flung open, looking out at the damage—smashed cars, lost roofs, twisted bikes, flooded yards—with a grand and easeful awe, the drizzle blowing in their faces. He felt as if he were in that very late painting of Gauguin's—he always mentions this part—the one with the royal pink sky in the background, and the bare-breasted maidens in it, who are gazing up mysteriously at something not pictured on the canvas itself. There are tropical vines in the background—for him these are the powerlines, snaking downward. He is supposed to be going to the corner, where Diana's brother Danny the deputy sheriff, out cruising to discourage looters, has agreed to pick him up, take him to the airport. He's planning to dash out onto the runway in the post-hurricane excitement, perhaps holding a sturdy airline umbrella, to board his flight, to escape to New England.

Diana says to him, "Andrew went over Livonia, it missed us by only this much," her papery little fingertips, which he would later learn to care for very much, pinched close together, but not quite touching.

He says, "Did it? Did we miss it?" He finds this hard to believe.

"The eye," she whispers, looking sideways at him, and down, crestfallen when she knows she shouldn't be.

The moment he likes most comes next: he takes her elbow to help her avoid the puddle right beside her—she could be electrocuted. In the same motion, feeling a kind of urgent glory, he picks up A. J. They head back down St. Helena away from where Danny should be waiting, back toward the women on their stoops, Diana's house. What he says to end the story is "And I just knew then." People here are satisfied with that.

It should have been a great disappointment to go back to the fresh chaos blown in on top of the kinds already in his life in Louisiana. He knew this. But he did and he's still there. He was overcome by a sweet homesickness for the very moment he was living in, just then—not the next, not one somewhere else. And the mysteriousness of it, how nothing ever followed. Such a feeling wouldn't travel to New England, much as he might like to take it. It was indigenous he thought; probably rare other places. He wouldn't be able to translate it. At the same time he was ashamed of himself, the delight he felt. Then he knew.

At a distance, the sirens.

# ABOUT THE AUTHOR

Moira Crone was born and raised in the tobacco country of Eastern North Carolina. She is a graduate of Smith College and Johns Hopkins University. The author of two previous books of fiction, *The Winnebago Mysteries and Other Stories* and *A Period of Confinement,* she has received grants from the Bunting Institute of Radcliffe College and the National Endowment for the Arts. Her stories have appeared in *The New Yorker, Mademoiselle, The Southern Review, Short Story,* and several anthologies, including *New Stories by Southern Women.* She teaches at Louisiana State University. The mother of two daughters, she has lived in South Louisiana for the last fourteen years.

*Library of Congress Cataloging-in-Publication Data*

Crone, Moira, 1952–

    Dream state / Moira Crone.

        p.   cm.

    ISBN 0-87805-813-3 (cloth : alk. paper)

    I. Title.

    PS3553.R5393D74   1995

    813'.54—dc20                   95-18249

                                CIP

British Library Cataloging-in-Publication data available